T0368721

Stories

MARILYN SHAPIRO LEYS

authorHOUSE®

AuthorHouse™
1663 Liberty Drive
Bloomington, IN 47403
www.authorhouse.com
Phone: 833-262-8899

Published by AuthorHouse   12/07/2022

ISBN: 978-1-6655-7727-4 (sc)
ISBN: 978-1-6655-7728-1 (hc)
ISBN: 978-1-6655-7726-7 (e)

Library of Congress Control Number: 2022922519

Print information available on the last page.

In Blackberry Season

E BUILT OUR LITTLE CABIN ON A RIDGE IN COULEE COUNTRY, three hours from the city's rush and flatness, where nights come early to the farms in the narrow valleys and the only pain's in blackberry season, when the arm that reaches in for the sweet fruit comes out with scratches.

Left to themselves, the thickets blanket a hillside with charitable swags, white in spring as bridal bush, in summer, green and head-high shady and dotted with tiny, profligate Christmas trees of ripe blue-black. Of course, to make more pastures, Bill Bennett had torn his berries out.

The Bennetts, Bill and Jane, were our first contacts in that county. The weekend after we closed on the land, they'd come bouncing up the dirt track bisecting our hill in their old pickup. Bill had been working on the roof of his new barn and had spotted us stacking the logs that would become our cabin's walls. Narrating, Jane pointed south to the next steep ridgetop, where a blue and yellow barn presided over several grey-red outbuildings and a small house. Jane was an impermanent blonde, her hair always in a french twist or a flip straight from a Sixties pattern book. Her clothes were antiques. Bill was almost always with her, a short, compact, sunburned presence, invulnerable and silent.

A day or two after that first meeting, when my men tired of watching me watch them work, they packed me off to the Bennetts' to solidify our acquaintance. This turned out to be an easy task. We sat at their kitchen table, Jane pouring iced tea, Bill drinking it, listening

1

to the first of her tales, then leaving me to listen to the remainder on my own.

They had moved to their farm two years before, Jane said, from a city where Bill had been a self-employed tinkerer. Two beautyshop-model hairdryers, three semi-fixed tv sets, car and tractor parts, one and a half police scanners--evidence that Bill had not totally abandoned his old life--littered the little room that was their kitchen and parlor. Over the six years I would know them, as Bill repaired things, sold them, bought more raw material at auction, their own worn furniture would appear and disappear beneath the rubble. Jane had been a waitress, but the other existence was gone, except for her eternal cheerful chatter. Now she seemed immersed in raising poultry, selling eggs, and tending the ever-increasing herd of steers Bill brought home from his auctions.

That first afternoon, Jane gave me the grand tour of the barnyard. Into the smaller paintless sheds she clumped, pushing aside gates fashioned from baling twine and peeled bedsprings she'd rescued from the township dump. She greeted her calves and cows and ducks and laying hens by the assorted names she'd given them in memory of some imperfection of behavior, or relative, or character in a book she'd read. Desiree, their milk cow, was her personal favorite.

The first day we set a pattern that would remain until last summer: I would appear; Jane would pour out iced tea and her monologues; Bill would drift in, sit down, drink tea, and leave. I would remain, lulled by the wash of words and the almost-silent peeping of the baby chicks Jane kept on the porch Bill hadn't finished. I always started out mildly amused, like a child listening to nursery tales, but then my attention would drift, and my mind would relax.

When Jane dropped by our cabin, knowing no other protocol, I served her tea. Our gas refrigerator provided the ice, for bringing electricity to that isolated ridge had proved to be too dear. So the refrigerator was new, and the Morso wood-burner, and the well and pump and generator. And the four-wheel-drive pickup we'd needed to haul things up the track. But other than those few things, the cabin was the stepchild of our city home. When we hauled in a couch that didn't match our new city carpet, Jane fretted that mice might chew it.

2

After we finished building, our city friends would drive out, camp out, share our outhouse and Jane's tales, while their kids petted Desiree or chased Jane's cats and chickens. But after a year or two, the kids became too old to be amused.

On the Bennetts' ridge, things were happening in their cycles: planting; buying bull calves and naming them and turning them to steers; haying; harvesting the oats and corn; sending steers to slaughter. And then there were the winter projects I'd miss out on, whose fallout still littered Jane's small house in planting time.

Jane first mentioned her daughter after three summers' visiting. From some deep reserve of names she hadn't squandered on her flocks and herds, she'd named her Euronda. Euronda was tossed in between the news that a tavern up the road had started buying Jane's eggs to serve hardboiled and an explanation I'd never need on how to cure some cow disease. Euronda had been packed off to an uncle in Wyoming, for reasons that I never knew.

There were times when Jane would stop in mid-flow to ask about my winter occupations or my life in the city. Occasionally she would ask my opinion about something she had read, or seen on whichever channel worked on Bill's current tv set, something almost always three years stale. Had I ever tried Chinese cooking? Were French wines all that superior? What did I think about this women's lib thing? And what was really causing all these divorces? Had I ever read Kurt Vonnegut? But she never left space for my answers, so I began to accept the questions as rhetorical, letting my mind drift since she did not seem to require any other response.

All this while, Bill had been acquiring more land, 300 acres across the road from their place, 160 acres next to ours. When he ran out of places to buy, he rented the ten flat acres behind our cabin to plant corn and, last summer, oats. He always paid cash for his land, and for the things he bought at auction. He owed no one, and never bought unless he could afford it. Said Jane, as Bill, smiling, nodded and sipped at her iced tea.

Over the years, the ruts in our dirt track deepened. Finally, last June, we hired a local contractor to grade the track and gravel it into the semblance of a road. But things move slowly there; the road was not finished until blackberry season.

Because my men were too busy to come with me, I arrived alone one Sunday evening. I began picking on Monday morning, wandering deep into the thickets, losing track of time as the bushes closed over my head. The bounty mesmerized me; I would think I had picked one path clean and another cluster of glistening blue-black would lure me forward. When I wandered out to get another bucket, my wrists were scraped and a little swollen where my blouse had failed to cover them. At noon, faced with two pails of berries, I decided to invite Jane over to share a pie and tea.

It had become very humid. At the Bennetts', I found Jane tugging at a seven-foot-high sheet of corrugated metal, trying to close an opening in the yellow and blue barn that Bill had never gotten around to securing more formally. To move the sheet required two pairs of hands, but Bill was gone, harvesting one of his fields.

A visit today would be impossible, Jane said, for there were tomatoes and grape juice and beans to can, and Bill had brought sixteen new calves home from the auction barn. His bargain had been unscheduled. Some of the calves just needed calming down, but two were sickly.

We pulled together at the metal sheet, a dump castoff, Jane confirmed. Feeling the need for a dose of her whimsy, I asked what she had named the calves. Jane shrugged; for now they would be known by the orange numbers in their ears.

As always, she walked me to my car and talked at me ten minutes more. I repeated my invitation; she stood, listening to the lowing of the new calves and the drone of a tractor somewhere down the ridge. At last she agreed to come the next afternoon at three o'clock. Three sharp.

Tuesday, when the sun woke me, there was a grey overlay across the sky. By midmorning, all blue was gone; by the time I had eaten lunch, a cloud shaped like Bill's plowblade, lifeless and inky grey, was overtaking the older greyness from the north. A fringe of pure white, like a slip that shouldn't show, bordered the blade of the plow. In all my visits, I had never seen such a cloud; moreover, every thunderstorm I'd ever watched had come marching toward me across the ridge that led to Bennetts' farm, the southern ridge.

The plow stirred the wind and the wind set the trees to muttering. Behind the cabin, Bill's oats bent almost flat. Then the long grass in front of the cabin bent down ahead of the wind, foot by foot down the hill, until everything behind me and ahead was bent.

The pie was cooling on the counter, the tea steeping in a pitcher on the table. By 1:30, the cabin had become so dark that I could only stand and watch the progress of the storm, afraid to light a lantern that might topple and set the place on fire.

After a very long pause, the rain came slicing down, obscuring my hillside, the valley, then Bennetts' ridge almost at the same instant. I do not know how long it rained and blew, but Jane arrived well before the storm let up, half an hour before she had agreed to come, on foot, and drenched.

She would not come inside until she had taken off the out-of-fashion calf-high leather snow boots she was wearing. Then, gingerly, holding the boot tops between her fingertips, she tiptoed across the oak floorboards to lay the boots on the metal tray beneath the woodstove. She asked for a towel and dried her streaming hair. Taking off her clear plastic raincoat, she begged forgiveness for wetting my cabin. Reluctantly, she sat on a chair I testified was waterproof, refused my offer of hot tea, accepted the cold drink, a piece of pie.

It had seemed like a nice day to take a walk down through her woods, across the valley, up my hill, she said. Until the storm broke, she hadn't seen it coming, for my hill obscured the plow-cloud. Half-listening, it did not strike me then that even I had read and understood the morning's greyness, and Jane had lived longer in that county, and much more thoroughly.

The monologue began after she had finished every crumb of pie, first an absent-minded compliment, then a complaint that last week, when Bill had driven up to check the oats, his tractor had left marks in my fresh gravel. She'd tried to clear away the tracks on her way up just now, she said, wiping the side of her foot across the cabin floor to illustrate her method.

The rest came tumbling out, then, standard stuff all tangled up with other things. New ducks, new chickens, her daughter in Wyoming, the son-in-law and granddaughter she'd never seen. The new part for Bill's latest tractor had been outrageously priced; she'd thought they might vacation in Wyoming last spring, but Bill explained they couldn't take the time. Our oats had looked good last week. Thinking of something, she snorted half a laugh and shook her head....

Four years, she answered. Euronda had been married four years last month. Her son-in-law was a good man, she guessed. Except he chose to live by scrounging odd jobs and fixing machines to sell. Euronda had reported that their house was cluttered, just like hers. There followed, then, the latest local gossip, long, detailed fairytales of people I had only met through Jane's words. Euronda had gone and married a man just like her father. Why?

When, later, I would have reason to recall that part, it was because of the unexpected silence as Jane stared at her glass. And the regret that burdened the question and hung in the silent air.

But then the flow picked up again, continued unrelenting, lulling me. The newest calves' lifespan at their place; Bill's latest project, a little car whose rusted body seemed its only fault. Jane had liked that little car, had even called Euronda to ask if her husband could scrounge a better body to wrap around the car's insides, which Bill had fixed. Jane liked that little car.

Bill sold it.

The storm blew off, blue sky appeared, and the now-cool air came seeping in. Jane got up and walked toward her boots, saying she'd better go. She pulled them on. Relatives had sent a package of clothes last week, she explained, indicating her jersey, slacks, the boots. These were probably out of style where the relatives lived, but seemed awfully fancy, being new to her. Not that they couldn't afford new clothes, but these were in such wearable condition. Bill said.

As the monologue trailed off, not really ending, Jane headed out my door. I watched her progress down the loose gravel; waving, I called goodbye. She turned back, called back an invitation to come for tea before I left, but then she paused and stared back beyond the cabin, toward Bill's oats. "They'll be lodged now," she said with such satisfaction that I found myself smiling. "Wrecked," she added. "Like somebody stomped them down." Realizing suddenly that her high-heeled boots were making square holes in my road, she did the best she could to brush away her marks with her foot as she continued down the gravel track. By late Wednesday morning, I'd filled every container we had with blackberries. I'd planned to stay longer, but the wet heat had returned, and with it, the grey overlay. Without Jane's chat to distract me, the greyness was seeping into me, leaving me with an unpleasant sense of foreboding and the certainty that I could not endure another storm like Tuesday's.

I was carrying the last of the berries to my car when Bill came up our road, pushing a little white motorcycle he'd rebuilt. He stood for quite a while, silently examining the logs of our cabin. Across the valley, his new calves were lowing. Reluctantly, he asked at last, "Did Jane seem strange to you yesterday?"

As I had only been a bystander, I considered the question briefly, then joked, "Not strange. Just wet." Bill was so silent, so still, that being alone with him began to make me uncomfortable I did not want to know, but I asked, "Why?"

"She left me this morning. I drove to town to pay the taxes. When I came back, she'd took the truck and gone. Left me a note that didn't make much sense, but that's her. You know how she is."

I did. Still, I wondered why he seemed to need to find fault with Jane at least as much as he needed to find her. He added, "Did she mention anything to you? You're the last one she saw, I guess."

Surely he was not trying to blame me, to make me share his guilt. It didn't fit. Their life on the ridge was something out of a storybook, like the tales of the unknown neighbors Jane spun when I came by. Surely the oncoming storm had made me edgy. And yet, an accusation lurked behind his appeal for facts, an accusation I did not deserve. For I was on vacation.

I thought back on what Jane had said yesterday. Subtracting the customary scramble, I remembered first the last thing she had mentioned, for, in all the years she'd talked at me, she'd never regretted anything that had passed into Bill's hands, been mended, slipped away. Except the little car.

Watching the cabin logs, Bill said, "I guess I knew that. But I told her it might not run more than a week." His face was turned away from me. I did not know if guilt was there or not. This time without a pause, he said, "Someone's coming over this afternoon to get the cattle. I can't handle that all myself and get the fields in, too. Jane knows that."

It was so matter-of-fact, so very cold. Surely Jane deserved better, some grief at least, to mark her going. I told him, "Jane mentioned something else besides the car. She mentioned Euronda, and the vacation you didn't take her on this spring."

At last he swung my way, but his face was impassive.

"She knew we couldn't get away," he said.

"Looks like she's decided she could, after all. Are you here to ask me where Jane's gone? She didn't tell me--believe it if you want to. But if I were you, I'd call Euronda."

Still the man showed no grief, no pain, looked only as if he'd stopped up on his way to see the oats. I was struck by the thought that in all the hours and hours of random conversation Jane had shared with me, she'd never shared, or tried to share, her pain. And now she was, although she'd done her best to wipe away the gravel traces. Her going had dragged me over their wall, into their box. It was not pleasant.

I let my anger out at last. I told him, "Jane mentioned yesterday that your son-in-law is just like you. And she can't understand why Euronda married such a man."

Bill did not say a word or make a sign of grieving, but when he had boarded his cycle, he kicked it sharply to a start, then wallowed off in the fresh gravel, quickly as he could, straight down our hill.

Leaving pain, long, long after the gravel dust was gone.

The Totem Pole

ABE GREEN WAS COUNTING HOUSES WHEN HE DROVE PAST THE alley. Beside him, on the spines of the seats, there balanced a log, swaddled in burlap. Abe Green turned toward it. "Imagine!" he opened. "A man puts in fifteen years on one street, and suddenly he has to count to find his own house! It starts a man thinking. And what's his conclusion? That there's not one other person on this street who doesn't also count houses at least once in a while. With," he added, "the probable exception of Maurice Levis."

Weekdays, Maurice Levis was a junk dealer, but every Friday night, after services ended, he appeared, like the phoenix, to conduct an Adult Education class of his own creating, a forty-minute venture into Jewish history, ethics, culture, religion, holidays, folklore, philosophy, humor, and cooking. To the log Abe Green explained, "Levis, I hasten to tell you, is a scholar. If you could see his house, it would look to you like any other house on this street. But inside the man is a whole set of different interests, and that makes him unique."

Before Green's eyes, two rows of row homes presented twin grey stone fronts, stretching from alleyway to alley, broken every twenty-five feet by a pair of white wooden doors and six white wooden window frames, one downstairs, two up, on either of the pair of homes. Fifty houses were on this street, the first like the third, the second like the fourth, on each side of the street twelve mirror-image twins and one odd. The two street-long green lawns were divided at every pair of doors by a concrete walk, which led

9

down five concrete steps to the common pavement, paralleling the street. Every unit was decorated with three tall pine trees in front of the parlor window and a solitary yew where the lawn began sloping toward the sidewalk.

"You might want to ask, 'If you don't like it, why don't you move?' but the simple fact is that in this city, if you are born into the row house class, you live there for the rest of your life. Or you spend five or eight thousand dollars more and you buy yourself a detached house, which looks like every other detached house on that street. And all you're getting is two more outside walls and bigger payments."

Abe Green eased his car into a parking space. He pulled a shovel from his side of the car and the log from the other. In five minutes he had dragged the log up the slope of his lawn to a spot in the center of the grass plateau. Ten minutes more, and the log was settled into a hole on the spot, with clots of sod surrounding it. The log was almost as tall as Green and twice as wide around.

Eva Green, coming down the street with the weekend groceries in her arms, took in, with one glance, her husband, the scattered sod, the shovel and the burlap-covered log. She broke into a jog, bouncing celery stalks and egg cartons high in their sacks. "My God, what have you got?" she shouted down the street.

Three old men, reading the evening paper on their front stoops, looked up at her.

Eva came up the steps, leaning heavily on the railing. She set her packages on the sidewalk. "I'm waiting," she announced.

"It's a surprise," Abe Green began.

"Yes."

"Turn around," he said, his face bright, "Turn around and shut your eyes."

"It's that bad?"

Abe Green ripped off the burlap covering. "You can turn around," he said.

His wife turned and stared. Her mouth fell open. "Where?" she said weakly.

Before her stood a redwood totem pole, five feet high. It bore a dozen wild creatures: bats and bears, wolves and eagles. Each beast had a set of glass eyes and was decorated in reds and oranges, greens and blues. Each beast stared off in a different direction. At the top of the totem pole was a woman with three wild eyes, four arms and, on her head, a dozen snakes in place of hair. She was painted black and green, and each eye was a different shade of red.

His wife began to sob. "My God, Abe Green, what have you done? Last time it was a horse you found wandering around the street, and the time before it was a cat with the mange and hair falling out all over the living room rug, and the time before that it was a dog you were keeping for a friend, with diarrhea. But did I complain? No, never. Not a word! But this? This the SPCA is not going to handle so easy!"

Abe Green sighed. "But what's wrong with it? It's genuine. A genuine nineteenth century American Indian totem pole."

"A genuine nineteenth century American Indian? Me, I've got a husband, he's a genuine twentieth century American shmoe. I'd like to plant him in the lawn, head first!"

Abe Green looked at his wife. He looked at the totem pole and stroked his chin. "What's wrong with it?"

She looked at him. "Well, for the first thing, she said, "nobody else has a totem pole."

She waited. Abe Green was silent.

"Well, what are you going to say to that?"

Abe Green looked up and down his street. He saw only grey stone, white wood and grass. He shrugged.

"Look, if it was only for my sake, maybe I'd let you keep it. But," she shifted her glance across the street, "with the rabbi practically a next door neighbor..."

"The rabbi? He doesn't know we exist. To him, we're just two more faces on Friday night."

"Don't be silly. He was asking after you just the other day."

"Oh? What did he say?"

"He said, 'How are you this morning, and how's the man of the house?'"

"That's very interesting."

"And also, my bridge club is coming here tomorrow."

"So?"

"Six days I've been preparing for this meeting, Abe. Cooking. Cleaning. Baking. The coffee alone. I paid twenty cents a pound extra for special coffee."

She rummaged beneath the celery until she found a much-gilded can, covered with lists of ingredients, testimonials and special offers, and capped, top and bottom, with removeable plastic lids. "Twenty cents a pound extra." She pointed to the totem pole. "With this in the front yard, they'll never even notice."

"So I'll give you the twenty cents!"

"Sixty. That's a three pound can. Mildred Greenspan's coming."

"Mildred Greenspan? You mean the mink-coat with the redone nose? I can hear it now...'OH what a LOVELY totem pole! Oh, when I think how I pleaded with my Bennie to get me one in time for my Herbie's bar mitzvah, which by-the-way-Stein-is-catering-for-five-thousand.'"

Her attention diverted by mention of the enemy, Eva picked up the thread. "It's not bad enough she talks like her kid's the only one that ever got barmitzvahed. The worst thing is, every time I find something new and different to do for Sonny's affair, I come to bridge club and she's already thought of it."

Abe Green's somber face brightened. "You could say the totem pole was bought for the bar mitzvah."

Eva scowled. Her attention focused again on the pole. "For what? I could tell her, for an instance, it's to stick in the little hot dogs on toothpicks?"

"You could ask the bridge club to come in the back door."

Eva snorted. "Listen, I have to make the dinner. You start figuring. And when you figure how to get this thing back where it came from, you can come in and eat."

"I'm not hungry!" he shouted to her retreating back.

"I'm not returning it!"

Eva entered the house. "I'm going to bed! Now!"

Abe Green stamped up the stairs to the house, crossed the living room, and stamped more emphatically up the stairs to the bedrooms. He stood at his bedroom window for five minutes, staring at the totem pole. A small breeze rose. One hundred fifty pines whispered in unison.

Abe Green lay down on his bed. He turned on his side, drew his knees to his chest, and pulled the covers more firmly over himself.

Presently, the front door slammed. It was Sonny, returning from school. His son shouted into the kitchen, "Hey Mom, where..."

Abe Green heard a pan slammed against the kitchen sink. "He's hiding in bed, the coward. Ask him yourself!"

Sonny raced up the stairs, two at a time, but halted abruptly at the door to the master bedroom. He whistled, then he said "Ah-ha!"

There was no response from the bed. "Ah-ha!" he repeated, with more expression, "a perfect fetal position."

Green straightened his legs, pulled the covers away from his face, and peered out at the doorway. "Hello, Sonny! Hello my bar mitzvah boy! Come in and tell me what you are talking about."

"The fetal position," his son said again, strolling into the bedroom. "You were in it."

"What is it?"

"It's how you were before you were born. It manifests an unconscious desire to return to the womb," said the twelve-year-old.

"Where do you learn such filth?"

His son sniffed, "Cripes, that's what we're having this week in Social Science. This term we do Sociology and Psychology, with some emphasis on Marriage Counseling. Last term we did the French language. It's all part of the school's new program, 'Brighter Horizons for Brighter Students.'"

"Doesn't say much for the duller students' horizons."

"Huh?"

"Just muttering. Listen, did your mother put you up to all this?"

His son pulled himself up straighter. "Pop, I'll tell you the truth, I couldn't be happier with your totem pole."

"Wonderful!"

Sonny took a small notebook from his jeans and sat down on the edge of the bed. "Yeah. Now I can use you for a case history. We have to get three case histories, typed up in duplicate, by next week."

He sat down on the bed and crossed his legs. "Now look, did you hate your mother?"

"Why?"

"Transference." His son nodded three times and pulled at his barren chin. "You might be transferring your hatred of your mother onto Mom. That's very common."

"She did put you up to this!"

"Look, Pop!"

"Let me give you a thing to think about, my pre-adolescent Freud," Abe Green said. "Consider this street, if you want to consider commonness. Fifty house, all alike. Fifty families living in them. And of those families, forty-nine are exactly alike too. Hasn't that ever worried you?"

"Pop..."

"Only Maurice Levis is different. Sure, on the surface he leads the same normal, the same humdrum existence as all the rest of us. But inside himself, the man is a mental gadfly, always occupied with some new adventure to lift him above it all. Sonny, I don't have his mental capacities, but I want to rebel too. And so I use props. Sonny, that totem pole is my ticket out of this grey world."

Sonny was scribbling in his book. When his father paused, he looked up, eyes agleam. "Hey, let's go into this attachment of yours for Mr. Levis. That'll really wow them in class!"

Suddenly, Eva was at the door. She broke in uneasily, "Sonny, Abe, look who's here."

Beside her, leaning against the doorjamb with arms folded at his waist stood the rabbi. "Abe," the rabbi muttered to himself.

Sonny snapped to attention. The rabbi walked into the room, stood at the foot of the bed and gazed solemnly at Abe Green. Then he pulled a chair up to the bedside and sat. "Shalom, Abraham," he said.

"What are you doing here?"

"I called him and asked him over," Eva said defiantly. "And he was good enough to come right away. So Abe, behave?"

Eva turned and walked out of the room. Sonny was staring openly at the rabbi. Eva returned to the bedroom door and motioned for Sonny to follow her.

The rabbi cleared his throat. "Actually, I did happen to notice the totem pole," he said. "I was walking home from synagogue, meditating, and I noticed the totem pole."

Abe Green was silent.

"Actually, your wife didn't call me. She called to me, you know. While I was standing and noticing the totem pole."

Abe Green rolled over onto his stomach and yawned, but when he looked out from under the covers, the rabbi was still seated, staring at him. A mournful expression was settling on his face. "Abraham, Abraham, what have you done? To make your wife cry out in sorrow? For what have you done this? Why have you planted a graven image on your front lawn?"

"Not a graven image, rabbi. Only a nineteenth century American Indian totem pole, genuine.

"It is a graven image Abraham, and graven images are against the highest Law. 'Thou shalt not make graven images.'" The rabbi coughed slightly, and folded the refolded his hands. "It's not a Commandment we use every day. Still, when the need arises it is there, Abraham."

"Look, to me it's not like the totem pole was something I was planning to danced around in a loincloth. You have to think of it as if it were a plaster swan or a cast iron lawn ornament. Except that this one happens to be wood, and bigger than most of them. I mean, doesn't intent count for something in Heaven?"

The rabbi was shifting to his next point without comment. "Abraham, Abraham," he intoned, "the voices of the prophets call out from the past to remove the totem pole from your lawn. The sages of the Talmud cry out to you in this hour. The totem pole, Abraham, it offends your ancestors." The rabbi raised his volume and solemnly addressed the ceiling with its myriads of lost souls who hovered there. "The thousands who died in the Inquisition and in the pogroms, have they all died in vain?" Now his pitch was higher too, and a melodic note had crept into his voice. "Are these all nothing to you, Abraham?"

Abe Green grunted softly. "You know, rabbi, I haven't heard you speak like this since last year when you were asking for the United Jewish Appeal. It's a real pleasure!"

The rabbi's eyes glittered. "Abraham, there is nothing in all my rabbinical experience to prepare me for this."

A smile broke over Abe Green's face. "Yes, isn't it wonderful? Imagine, a plain man like me. From a man like my neighbor Levis, a learned man, you might expect such a thing, but from me?"

"Maurice Levis," said the rabbi haughtily, "would never break a Commandment. No matter how obscure."

The rabbi walked out of the room and Eva walked in a second later. "Did the rabbi talk to you?"

"What else?"

"I mean, did he get anywhere?"

"By now, I imagine, he's almost home."

She sighed again and wiped a tear from the corner of her eye. Abe Green silently curled himself into a knot, remembered Sonny's theories, and uncurled himself.

"I happened to hear you mention Maurice Levis," Eva offered timidly. "Would you want to talk to him?"

Abe Green meditated. "I don't think it could hurt anything," he said at last.

His wife went downstairs to the telephone. In five minutes, there was a knock on the front door. Then Maurice Levis materialized beside the bed, silent and very serious. Abe Green hesitated. The man had lived three doors away for years, but their only contact had been in the class, and there Abe Green had been one of thirty students. He ventured, "Hello."

"Hello," said Maurice Levis.

Abe Green searched his mind. "How's business," he asked.

"Horrible." For the first time, Levis smiled. "In June things are always horrible." He leaned forward and confided, "There's a definite trend to my business, and a reason behind it, too. I have a theory about that."

Abe Green stared at the man's red plaid bermudas. "About the junk business?"

"Why not?" Levis put on a pair of horn-rimmed spectacles. "Look at it like this: in June, people begin planning their summer vacations. And suddenly, everybody gets very careful about the way they use their cars. That's so they'll be in good shape for vacation. Now what does this do to me? Me, a junk dealer? It knocks the bottom out of my inventory. I'll bet you that every year, the accident rate goes down two hundred per cent in June.

"And then what happens?" Levis sobbed under his breath. "Comes

July, they take their cars a thousand miles away. They get to looking at all the trees and the flowers and all the new places. They get busy and then they have a smashup. And then, some stranger gets the junk!" Levis sobbed more audibly. "I tell you, it's a hard life for a Jew."

Incredulously, Abe Green asked, "You think there's some sort of anti-Semitism involved?"

"Absolutely!"

There was a dead silence.

Then the junk dealer brightened again. "If you'd like to hear it, I have another theory." He paused. "Actually, this one isn't my theory. I mean, I couldn't take credit for a theory so deep. Actually, this one comes from a learned journal I've been reading. I wouldn't bring it up, except..."

Abe Green smiled a bitter smile. "Except this is the one you really came here to talk about?"

"Yes, well...can I continue?"

Abe Green waved his arm regally. "Be my guest."

"It's all about what the historians call Assimilation. That's a general term. In this article I was telling you about they get down to cases. They call it, Misplaced Ethnic."

Abe Green stared at him.

"I'll make it simple for you. I see it like this: we all try to go back to our roots, right? It makes you secure. Now take you, for instance. You, obviously, have assimilated nicely into the American Way of Life. You have a house, a car, a son who's being bar mitzvahed. Only thing is, like the Hellenists of old, you have gone a bit too far. The ancestors you chose to go back to are not Ours. You went back to the ancestors of this country. In short, the Indians. A clear case of Misplaced Ethnic." Levis nodded emphatically, then he continued, "but you know what happened to the Hellenists."

"When class ended last month, we were in Egypt."

"The way I see it, I mean, this is my own theory now, it's due to an overdose of George Washington in our school system."

"George Washington?"

"George Washington, Abraham Lincoln, the whole rigamarole. Too much of Their history, not enough of Ours. If you want to talk about the Indians, why, I bet you were never even taught that there were Jews along with Sitting Bull at the Battle of the Little Big Horn! And that's not the only thing." Levis shifted from foot to foot. "Look, I hate to say this, but," his voice dropped to a whisper, "I don't think your totem pole is real."

"What do you mean?"

Levis regained his composure. "You know I'm a student of history. Well, in my reading I've seen many pictures of totem poles. Maybe even thousands. And not a single one has had a woman on top."

"Levis, have you seen a picture of every totem pole there is in the world?"

"No, I don't think so. But what has that got to do with it?"

"Nothing, and that's just the point." Suddenly, Abe Green could feel the wet heat of the evening bearing down on him. "Levis, when I knew you were coming, I said to myself, here comes somebody who's going to understand me, a brilliant man, a scholar. But you don't understand. Not at all!" Abe Green pulled the covers over his head.

"But I just told you that I do understand. Your problem isn't unique. There are quite a few historical precedents. The German Jews, for instance..."

"Levis, all I wanted was a little decoration for my lawn, a little something to say to the world, 'This is Green's house.' It happened that this totem pole caught my eye at that moment. Now, if you really think I should put up a big gold Star of David on my lawn, well, I'll think about it."

"That's not what I meant!"

"Oh, Levis, you were my last hope. Surely, I thought, Maurice Levis will intercede with my wife. Surely, he will be my saviour."

Suddenly Levis clapped his hand to his forehead, jumped up and ran for the stairs. "Don't stop me anybody!" he yelled. "Right now! I've got to write this to the learned journal right now!"

"What?" Abe Green hollered after him.

"A genuine Double Misplaced Ethnic!"

Now it was dark. Abe Green lay on his back and watched the pattern of passing lights on the ceiling. "Is there nothing left?" he said to himself. "Nothing in the world?"

He heard his wife talking on the telephone. Then she came upstairs. She lay down heavily on the bed. He turned to her with an explanation on his tongue, but she turned away.

Abe Green lay and listened to the cars. Shortly, one pulled up near his house. There was the sound of two voices, a thud, and after ten minutes the car roared away.

In the morning the sun was shining. Abe Green rose and looked out of the bedroom window. He looked down and down. There was no totem pole. As if by magic the totem pole had disappeared and the lawn was smooth and resodded.

His wife woke and sat up. "They paid us fifty dollars. We can put that toward Sonny's bar mitzvah." She smiled. "You didn't even have to do any of the work yourself."

Abe Green turned on her. "After so many years!" he cried. He threw on his shirt and trousers and ran out of the house.

The day passed slowly for his wife. By dinnertime, Abe Green was not at home. He was not home at seven o'clock or at eight. At nine o'clock, Sonny suggested that they call the police, but his mother said, "A paddy wagon is all we need."

Eva sat alone until midnight. Sometimes she sobbed. Sometimes she said to herself, "Why did he do such a thing? How could he do this to me? In front of all our neighbors?"

Then she went to bed and fell asleep.

She awoke early the next morning and reached to the other side of the bed. It was empty and the sheets felt very cold. It was still dark outside, or so it seemed, but the radium hands on the clock read seven. She ran to the window and looked out.

The entire bedroom window was blocked by what appeared to be an immense, two-headed bear. She looked up and down. Before her, above her, below her, was a totem pole, thirty feet high, carved from ebony and painted five different shades of seven different colors. Not a single surface had been left uncarved. There were vampire bats and bears and seals and porpoises and eskimos, male and female. In between these larger creatures were snakes and small, evil-looking birds and hundreds of insects.

And at the foot of the totem pole, blissfully asleep under the seven-foot-wide span of a vulture's wings, was Abe Green, his arms wrapped as far as they would stretch around the pole.

Eva shrieked. At the sound, Sonny bounded out of his room and raced to the window. He looked up and down and whistled softly. "Wait till I report this in class. What a phallic symbol! Hey, Ma, where do you think he got this one?"

"Don't look at me," she sobbed.

"And how did he get it up there?"

Eva had nothing to contribute.

"Hey, Ma, maybe we should have let him keep that other one?"

"Listen, your father is like a little child, you have to do for him. So don't accuse me, because I only did the best for him."

Sonny was about to speak.

"Breakfast will be ready soon," she interrupted, still sobbing. "So get washed up and then go wake your father. He must be hungry by now."

Sailing

ERNIE IS A ROYAL PAIN IN THE ASS. HE MAY BE MY AUNT'S youngest brother in law, but he's also a kvetch, a constant and unremitting whiner. And the worst of it is, he whines about one thing only, his wife's father. Or he talks constantly about his sailboat. Which is no improvement, if you're not a sailboat freak. He's like a kid who's just learned to play the violin and has only been taught two notes so far-- and poorly, at that.

But he was the only familiar face I saw in the room, and I was not at all sure about my father's theory of strangership.

Bernie's father in law was a shill for the gastroenterologists, Bernie said. The problem, and how could I forget, was that the man gave advice. "Whenever I know he's coming, I have to quick fix up everything in the house," Bernie said. "Otherwise, my father in law's right on me. And if I'm not around at the time, my wife gets the advice and passes it on." And it wasn't just the advice, it was the manner in which it was presented. "If you'd get me a board, I'd..." or "Get me a little rug cleaner and I'll..." "The implication is that I'm a lazy bum who does nothing but lay around, while he's the Boy Scout, going to fix up my whole life," Bernie has said, more than once. "A couple times, I made the mistake of taking the advice on the spot, and I started fixing the stuff right away. And there he was, hanging over my shoulder, I mean actually breathing in my ear. I'd turn a screw and he'd go 'Hmmm.' I'd keep on turning and he'd go 'Uh oh'. Then it was all I could do not to tell him what he could do with it. But my wife always plays the

21

diplomat. 'He's been like that all my life,' she says. 'It's his way of being helpful, of feeling useful, powerful. We all have our own little ways. What do you want from his life?' she asks. 'He's an old man. He's not going to be around much more. Then you'll have all the rest of your life to not be bothered.'"

Fortunately for Bernie's tender stomach, his in laws lived a thousand miles away. Unfortunately, his father in law had retired several years before, but his mother in law was still working. Consequently, there were times when he would visit alone perhaps twice a year, adding fuel to Bernie's complaints. Which he had a habit of airing to me at family gatherings.

And here he was again his lips working in and out. "Hey, Bern," I said in greeting. "How's it going?"

"Not so hot."

"Your father in law again?"

"Yeah. I guess so."

"Visiting?"

"Sort of."

"Sort of? What does that mean?"

"Good question."

He fell absolutely silent. His lips worked in and out again. "So tell me, I got all the time in the world," I said, turning the volume on the tape recorder up slightly.

"Well, you know about me and the old man. I guess I've bored you often enough telling you about my troubles with him. I swear to you, I love that old man very much, although mostly when he's not around but every time he visited it was the same thing: not only why don't you do it, but do it like this, one two and three. My stomach would start to knot up two, three days before he was due, and when he came it would be a regular hardball, and it would burn and keep shooting up through my throat to the top of my head. I wanted to punch him, or at least yell 'Stop it! Shut up! I'll do it my own way, when I feel like doing it.' But my wife would always be there to catch me. And my father in law? He never noticed a thing. He'd always sit there, in my favorite chair, no less, eating up all my son's cookies, with his hands folded across his belly and smiling, like he'd just done me the greatest favor in the world and I'd think to myself, 'Some day, old man, you're going to find out you're not so smart after all. And that will shut you up!' Yes, that's what I would think." Bernie paused again, and his lips worked in and out again. What was this? I thought to myself. The words were the same, the content was the same as always. And yet the usual bitterness was tinged, no drenched, with a distinct note of regret.

"But there was one part of my life that he hadn't pried into until two summers ago, and that was my boat." Here it comes, I thought, and yawned to myself. "I guess I've bored you enough with that too," he said. That was a surprise, I thought. Most unBernielike.

"But my wife was a diplomat where I was concerned too. Everytime he'd make noises about wanting to go, she'd find something else for him to do. I think my wife knew that a few suggestions about fixing leaks and cracks and putting up extra shelves I could take. Especially since, underneath, I knew that my father in law was competent in those areas. But the boat was the one thing he knew absolutely nothing about, absolutely nothing. Hell, you should watch him & my mother-in-law walk down a sidewalk. They warn each other to be careful every time there's a curb! Anything wilder than that, my father-in-law usually makes his excuses & stays home & takes a nap.

But then, one day last summer, while he was paying a visit alone, my wife left us. She went to the store or something. My son and I were trying to sneak out of the house while he was napping in my chair and get down to the boat before he caught us. But it didn't work." He paused again and looked off. I waited and waited. Nothing. "So?" I said, to sort of nudge him off his memories.

He sighed, like an ancient, rusty machine winding up, and began again. "My father in law woke up and looked around. 'Where you going?'

"'Probably to the boat,' I said, hoping that the annoyance in my voice would transmit. It didn't. 'Can I come? I always wanted to come. I always tell everybody my son in law's got a boat and they always say how is it and I always gotta say..well, I guess okay.'

"That sort of got to me. 'Okay, come, but you have to have tennis shoes or something,' I told him.

"'Hey, I got a regular yachting outfit. I bought it right after Sara wrote that you got the boat. I been bringing it out every summer, but...'

"'Okay." I said. 'Okay. Okay, 'Get it on and lets get going.'

"Within two minutes he was out again. 'How do you like my boating regalia?' he said.

"Oh my god," I said, to myself, I hope. The outfit consisted of a white jersey sports shirt, with two large boating type flags criss crossed across the pocket, a pair of navy blue pants, and to match, one of those phony navy blue yachting caps with the crossed gold anchors on the brim and yards and yards of gold braid circling the edges all the way around. But beneath it all was the pièce de resistance, so to speak. Instead of the tennis shoes I'd requested, for some reason he had chosen to wear high-topped gym shoes with white rubber edging and white eyelets and white laces, very long, very white and double knotted. Now, you have to remember how my father in law looks: he's got a big belly but very, very skinny legs. So the belly had the pants hiked way up, and there were those high tops, in all their splendor. God, don't let any of my enemies see me today, I remember praying under my breath. But what he said was "You ought to get yourself an outfit like this. Look nice." And he looked disapprovingly at the old sports shirt & jeans I'd chose for today's outing.

"It was a clear day when we started out, my ten year old, my father in law, and I. The breeze was very light then, so light that for a while I thought we'd have to turn the motor on to get back home. The suggestions, of course, began right away. You know how the Marina is. There's a long, wide pier going out to the boats and then between each two boats there's a narrow finger pier. Well I guess there's a fairly big step down from the main pier to our pier, but we've always just stepped down. Never noticed it. But he starts in, why don't I rig a wooden step so it wouldn't be so hard to step down. If I measured so it was half as high as the distance from one pier to the other and then....But by this time my son and I had slimbed onto the boat and were waiting to help him aboard. I reached out a hand and he starts in again, why don't we build up steps from the pier to the boat, he's seen some going up to the big motor boats across the way. If I want, he'll take me over there and show me before we leave the dock. Or a gangplank. How about a gangplank? But I'm standing on the cockpit seat, and I keep pushing my hand out at him and I guess I look pretty forbidding or something, so he finally gives me his hand and I haul him aboard. He's getting his balance on the seat and hanging onto the boom. 'Dirty,' he says, looking around and clicking his tongue. 'If you get me a sponge and a bucket...'

"'Yeah, Pop,' I say. 'It's early in the season yet. I haven't had a chance to clean it up yet so early in the season. But it is getting late in the day, you know what I mean?' I was feeling pretty grim what with all his looking around and chattering, we'd already been at the dock fifteen or twenty minutes, and he hadn't gotten settled in the cockpit yet. I jumped down off the cockpit seat and started unfastening lines. Very slowly, very carefully, he sat down on the seat and swung his legs onto the floor.

"Like I said, the breeze was very light when we started out. That is something I want to get clear, right now. Whatever else I ever did wrong to that man, I never took him out knowing...."

"Knowing what? Knowing what?" I prodded. So much mystery from Bernie, with so little content, was getting on my nerves, but I was determined to be a good listener.

And again he began. "My father in law was quiet, very quiet at first. At the time I thought it was simply that he was in awe of the way you can go in a sailboat when things are just right, smooth and fast, and yet in absolute silence. 'How do you like it?' I ventured, after a long spell of his silence began getting on my nerves. I prayed that I wouldn't be answered by a suggestion. But he only nodded, smiling a little. He adjusted his cap tighter on his head, so that the braid almost came down to his ears. I asked him if he'd like to steer for awhile, since we were running with that weak wind behind us, and there wasn't much he could do wrong. I thought that last thing, but I didn't say it. I'd swear to that. But he just shook his head without saying a word. My son, all this while, was sitting on the foredeck, stretched out and getting a tan, enjoying the smooth, flat ride. After perhaps twenty minutes of this uncharacteristic silence, my father in law cleared his throat. 'This is nice, real nice.' More silence, then, 'You sure wouldn't have caught my father doing something like this.' Here it comes again, I thought to myself, how his father came over from Russia and had to work day and night at the business and never had time for 'the finer things' as he always said. But he didn't say that. Instead, he said, simply, 'Thank you for letting me share your boat.'

Then he fell silent again. We sailed on silently for almost an hour. I had the boom way out, and a rope vang holding it down to the rail. Then I decided we'd better have some lunch and start back home, since I knew we'd have to tack all the way back.

I asked my father in law to reach in the cooler to get the soda and sandwiches, but he just kept starting at the white expanse of mainsail. So I called my son down from the foredeck and we got the lunch out together. My father in law accepted a sandwich and soda without comment. He didn't, and this surprised me, even think to warn my son to be careful to put his sandwich wrapper in the garbage and not to cut himself on the can.

I was balancing the tiller on top of my foot, popping open my soda, when there was another dull pop behind me. I turned around and found that as the knot on the vang had worked itself loose, a sudden gust of wind had caught the sail and pulled the boom free of the rope. It was only one gust, I told myself. The wind seemed calm enough otherwise. But I suggested that we finish up and start for home. As we were stowing the garbage, it became apparent to me that this was not a stray gust, after all.

'Uh oh, looks like the wind is really up,' my son observed. 'Hey Pop, maybe you ought to take down the jib so we don't have such a fast ride home.' My father in law looked stricken. My son, turned to him and said, 'It's gonna be a real sleigh ride, Grandpa!'

Fortunately, for my son, I was already standing on the cabin top, unfastening the jib halyard; otherwise, I might have said something nasty to him. I could only guess what my father in law was thinking at this point. It was when I got to the foredeck to take in the sail that I noticed the boat beginning to pitch. So what, I thought. The boat can handle it. That's why I bought a boat with a big heavy keel. She was a stiff boat, I knew it and my son knew it. So what?

I came down into the cockpit and took over the tiller from my son. We came about and I started the boat off in approximately the direction we wanted to go. The wind had really come up and the boat was staring to heel. I looked at the cabin top, which was standing at a slight angle to the water and I braced myself for the suggestions. Why didn't I do something with that stick and get the boat straight up again, like it was before? Wouldn't it be more comfortable if the boat was riding straight in the water?

But the suggestions didn't come, and when I turned around to look at my father in law, I found him staring down at the water in a way that made me feel uneasy. I'd better explain, I thought. If nothing else, maybe it will head off the suggestions. After all, I told myself, feeling charitable, my father in law the expert has never been in a sailboat before. Why should he understand, just like that? So, as cheerfully as I could, although I was on edge from anticipating, I said, 'Heeling is something a sailboat is designed to do.'

"And he said, smiling a silly smile, 'I thought heeling was something you teach a dog.' Oh, God help me, I thought, and dropped it.

The wind was blowing from the wrong direction entirely, and it was blowing hard. The waves were starting to build and the boat was pitching perceptibly. Instead of moving south, which was what we wanted, the boat would only go east, west or northeast. We were getting nowhere. "Let's turn on the motor," I told my son. 'Maybe we can get her pointed into the wind that way.'

"'You mean you don't know for sure?' said a very small voice from the other side of the cockpit, and at that, a finger of wind lifted his cap and sent it well across the lake.

My son turned the motor on and I turned the boat south. As soon as he pushed the motor to forward, the boat responded. The mainsail filled, the dacron stretching taut, and we plowed into the waves. But the boat was heeling until one rail was in the water. My father in law, still holding onto the place where his cap had been, was sitting on the low side of the boat, looking straight into the depths of the lake. No good, I thought. 'Come sit up here near the cabin, on the high side of the boat,' I said.

No response.

'Come sit up here next to me,' I yelled, offering my hand. Wordlessly, he groped his way up the cockpit, and I dragged him onto the seat beside me. A shower of spray hit us all, and my father in law brushed it out of his hair. Then a large wave of spray hit us. My father in law moaned; he grabbed for the cabin with both hands. I saw him looking down at the low rail, and I looked too. It looked like a long way down. The rail was in the water all the way and the boat appeared to be about to tip over. Above us, the mainsail stretched and stretched until, it seemed, the dacron would have to tear apart. Behind us, the motor was grinding away, wailing as it came all the way out of the water, and moaning as it fell back in again. If I didn't know the boat could take it, I thought to myself, I'd worry. But I wasn't about to tell him, I thought. I'm not in the mood for another snappy answer. It was then that my son chose to say, 'Don't worry, Grandpa, it's fun. It's just like the roller coaster.' My father in law turned to look at him, and was about to smile when my son, who was still sitting on the low side of the boat leaned well over the rail, dipped his hand into the water and said, 'See, nothing to worry about.' My father in law moaned again, and put his cheek to the side of the cabin. His left hand gripped the cabin opening convulsively, while his right hand clutched a cleat. His eyes were forward, but large sheets of spray kept hitting him square in the eyeglasses, and I doubted that he could see, even if he was focusing.

The wind was growing worse and worse, and though I knew that the sail was helping us move along, and though I knew the ship could take it, I was aware that I was becoming more tense and more uncomfortable each minute. Besides, it suddenly struck me, my father in law's position at the cabin coaming was a silent suggestion in itself. 'Do something!' he seemed to be crying out. 'Get this thing fixed!' The tension grew in me as the boat plowed along, fighting the wind and making very little headway. Finally I gave up. 'Okay,' I said to the other two. 'I'm going forward to get the mainsail down.' I turned to my son, saying, 'You take the tiller.'

I crawled up to the top of the cabin, stood, and braced my feet. I uncleated the mainsail halyard and was just about to start letting the sail down when an even stronger burst of wind hit us, along with a wave of very cold water. The surface I was standing on grew slippery. I had seen that wind coming, had seen the waves breaking up into tiny pocks, as if they were being hit by raindrops, though the sky was mockingly, cloudlessly blue, and I had found myself praying, wind, hold off till I get down. The boat bent further into the water, and then, at last, I heard the voice. It was directed at me and it said, 'Do something! You do something! Take that stick and steer it right. He's only a baby. He'll never do it right!'

Something snapped in me. 'You do it then! I yelled. You know how to do everything!' Years and years of accumulated suggestions came tumbling about my feet as the mainsail fell in folds over me. I was cut off from the world, and especially from my father in law, and despite all the dacron on top of my body, I felt lighter than I had ever felt in my life. A wet white cloud kept me from seeing the old man's face, but frankly, at that point anyway, I couldn't care less.

As soon as the pressure of the wind was off the sail, the boat righted itself. The roaring of the wind in the sail was gone and the motor, now remaining for longer periods of time in the water, was purring. But my father in law was sitting in the cockpit, his hatless head bent, his hands clasped between his knees.

When we got back to shore, he said nothing. He got into the car and said nothing. I purposely went through a yellow light while he was watching, but he said nothing.

He stayed at our house for one more night, as had been arranged, but he didn't make a single suggestion. When my wife asked him where he'd gone that day, he said, 'Nowheremuch.' And then he left. My mother in law says, when he got home, he just sat around for a good week. Wouldn't talk. Wouldn't eat, not even cookies. Then he seemed to come to life a little bit. At least he'd answer questions, which he hadn't done up till then. The next time he came, with his wife, and he never came alone again, and every time one of them wanted something, it was she who asked. I had to admit to myself that the old man, I mean the old old man, had at least been alive. This version was a zombie, who just sat in my chair, napping, always napping, until I would walk by. Then he would rouse himself, stare at me, and touch his head where the cap had been. He'd usually start to say something, but then he'd stop himself, and fall into a nap again.

So I keep asking myself, did I kill the man? I mean, granted, he's not dead, but it's as if the backstay on a boat had snapped in a high wind, just that one thin wire snapped, but that made the whole mast come tumbling down. Am I some kind of murderer? That's what I keep asking myself. And then I say to myself, next time you leave the revelations to God. And then I say to myself, but the wind was light when we started out that day. We were almost becalmed. How could I have known? And then I say, excuse me, but I was under tensions, up there on top of the cabin. I'm always under tension when he's around. And then I say..."

Like I told you at the beginning, Bernie is a royal pain in the ass.

At the top of the stairs was a grocery store, a space, a bakery, another space, and a two door, two story fading yellow house. Over one of the doors was a large wooden sign indicating that the United States Post Office had a home inside. The sign itself was hand lettered, but various standardized red, white and blue stickers on the windows linked the office with thousands of standardized other. A hand lettered sign on durable cardboard was tacked to the second door. "Aunt Ella's Museum," it said, "come in, it's WARM inside."

As John was about to rush them all past, the second door opened and a white-haired woman stepped out. "Come in," she beckoned, "it's warm inside."

Before John could stop her, she had wrapped one arm about Jackie's shoulder and was guiding the boy inside. Richie followed, and Ruth after them. "Reminds me of the old witch and the gingerbread house," John muttered.

"Shut up!" Ruth whispered.

Directly ahead of them was a staircase. To their left was a door into the post office. The old woman opened a door to their right and they all followed her inside. The room they stood in was fairly large, but every wall was covered with things, and things stood all around the room, filling a border of at least two feet of floor space next to every wall. On the wall next to the door was a daybed and beside the daybed was a small table with very old pitcher and basin and a hand lettered sign on durable cardboard which read, "Your donations are my only salary. Twenty five cents suggested. Children free." Beyond the daybed was a second door which was open. Beyond that door was a second room, another daybed over which hung an enormous ancient quilt. That bed was flanked by tall, narrow windows, which looked out on the black granite boulders and the rushing creek. There were windows also in the first room, but these admitted only a little light, for they were hung with ancient lace curtains, on which were pinned additional things. "My God!" John whispered, "I feel like I'm standing at the bottom of a wastebasket."

Ruth pursed her lips and exhaled. "Shh."

The old woman sighed. She was of medium height and her shoulders were only slightly bent. When she spoke, her voice was free of the quavering of age, but it seemed that this was a result of deliberate effort on her part. She wore a hand crocheted grey wool skirt with a well defined scallop pattern, which fell almost to her ankles, an old fashioned white blouse with reddish small polka dots and a garnet colored woolen shawl. "It's certainly cold outside," she said, drawing her shawl closer to her chin, "but it's nice and warm in here."

Jackie was staring at the things on the wall. "Well, now, would you like to hear me play my musical saw? That's what I'm famous for around here, don't you know."

"Can you really play a saw?" Jackie asked.

"I played it on national television once," the old woman replied. She nodded at the wall above the china pitcher, where a series of photographs hung. "I was on the Johnnie Carson show. I was on with Liberace."

Indeed, one photo depicted the old woman, slightly younger, her lips fixed in a flirtatious smile. Beside her was the pianist; beside him, the ubiquitous candelabra; on her knee, a saw. Another shot had her standing beside Carson, disdainful smile on his lips, saw on her knee. For the first time in his life, John felt a comradeship with the cynical television star.

The old woman disappeared into the second room and came back carrying an ordinary looking hand saw and a cello bow. She sat down on an armless chair, quite near the hand lettered sign, and tucked the wooden handle of the saw under her right knee. Suddenly her knee began a palsied shaking. Her left hand, meanwhile, was bending the tip of the saw, up and down, while her right hand waved the bow beyond the toothed edge of the saw. The shaking knee and the moving hands continued their motions for perhaps five seconds, then, from nowhere, there arose a disembodied ghostlike howl. It shocked John, for he could not place its source. Soon, however, it resolved itself into a howling melody, and he realized that the old woman's left hand seemed to be

31

moving up or down, a few seconds before the pitch went up or down. The old woman was playing the "Star Spangled Banner." As "the home of the brave" drifted away toward the things on the curtains, Jackie began to applaud. Richie joined him, and Ruth. John pitched two quarters into the old jug. They clanked. "Thank you," said the old woman. John started toward the door.

"I played my saw on television on my eighty second birthday, don't you know," the old woman said coyly.

"How many years ago was that?" Ruth asked.

"Four. I'm eighty six now, and proud of it."

"Today is my father's birthday," Jackie said loudly.

"Is that so well, we must play "Happy Birthday" then. Now what is your father's name?"

"John."

"Well, I'll play, and then we'll all sing." The knee began its palsied shaking, the right hand its mysterious waving, and there emerged into the air the howling, this time resolving itself into "Happy Birthday." John stood rigid near the door. Jackie and Richie and the old woman sang the words in the same piping voice. Ruth's voice was low pitched and loud. "Oh my god," John moaned.

When this ended, the old woman placed her saw and bow carefully in the corner near the door to the second room. "Well, I suppose you'd like to see my museum," she said. "Now, I'll bet you'll never guess what I have behind this door." She flung the door shut with a dramatic notion and there on a hook was a pair of white breeches, tapered at the calf. "These are George Washington's breeches," she said, "or at least they were made in George Washington's time. Just look at all the handwork on these. Handmade buttons, handmade cloth. So old, but it will last forever."

"Looks like the same twill my Navy whites were made of," John muttered.

"Will you shut up?" Ruth hissed.

Jackie stroked the heavy white material, then dropped his hand reluctantly. Gently the old woman reopened the door, hiding, in addition to the breeches, four old hats, three rusty umbrellas a small quilt and several photographs which hung on the wall behind the door.

From a nail on the wall to the right of the doorway, the old woman took a baby's dress of yellowed white cotton, elaborately tucked and decorated with yellowed handmade lace. "This was my own brother's dress," she said. "My, these things are old."

"Christening dress?" Ruth inquired.

"No, he wore this till he was three, don't you see."

Jackie gasped. "Why did he do that?" he asked.

The old woman looked puzzled. "But everyone did, boys and girls. It was a long time ago."

"Probably made it easy to get to the wet diapers," John suggested.

The old woman hung the dress back on its nail gingerly. "That could well be," she conceded. "Now, here is what I imagine to be the prize of my collection." She moved to a black lace shawl which was spread on the wall above a small, littered table. Although it might have been valuable to her, it too was surrounded by things - additional small dresses, babies' bonnets, women's feathered hats and several fans.

"This was handmade in Spain, a very long time ago. My husband and I saw the women making these when we were on our honeymoon. They would sit in the bright sunshine with pillows on their laps. On the pillows would be placed tiny pins, and by weaving the threads in and out between the pins, the women would make this beautiful lace. Many women went blind making these. They are called mantillas."

"Probably didn't get any workman's compensation either," John remarked.

The old woman paused. "They probably didn't," she finally acknowledged. "Now, here is something else I'd like to show you," she said, moving right again. It was a red fox, with a large ring through its nose. The ring was hung on a nail. "I was driving my car to the village one day and I saw this run into the road in front of me. I couldn't stop the car in time, don't you see. But when I finally did get the car stopped, why, I walked back and picked him up and took him to have him prepared."

"How many years ago was that?" John asked.

"Was what?"

"That you were driving?"

"Shut up," Ruth whispered.

"Not too many."

The decor was Early American; the artwork, Late Jesus.

That was all Richard registered before the mullioned rectangular peephole swung aside and he was faced with Mickey- and Minniemouse. Minniemouse simpered "Happy Halloween" at him and Mickeymouse danced a little jig in time to the wiggling of her finger. Richard's eye was caught by her chartreuse legs.

He was still watching the legs when the other voice said, "Hello, Richard, come on in," and now he was facing Dickie Prize with a mask in his hand, otherwise known as the <u>News</u>' enterprising managing editor. Not enterprising in his hustle after news--though it wasn't fair to judge after two weeks. He'd only been working here two weeks. Enterprising in what? What was one's enterprise when one was named managing editor at thirty-two? How did one rise from assistant city editor at the other paper, to the managing editor at this one in one swift upward bound. Was Dickie as good at bounding as his wife was at dancing? Better--he'd have to be one hell of a lot better. In any case, this was clearly a pass the peace pipe party--decorate it up with all the orange and black streamers in the world and you still couldn't disguise it. For over there, drinking Dickie's booze, was one man who'd been passed up, and in another corner, under a highly colored picture of the moneychanger being chased, another. Booze! Didn't the idiot know better than to show off like that. On the peons' wages they all got--maybe not Dickie Prize, but certainly everybody else in the damn room--nobody served booze at a party. Nobody served beer. It was strictly bring your own--and beer was the best that anybody had.

The pick up on parking near the bridge--which is near the paper, and the downtown shopping. Have a discussion between wives and husbands about whether it's safe to be there.

"All they're going to do is panhandle you," Dickie says. "Nobody has the energy left to do anything else." It's the booze, the booze gets into you and replaces your energy." "What are you worried about, rape?" Richard asks a particularly fat wife.

Dickie is annoyed. "You don't even have to worry about purse snatching," he tells her, putting his arm around her.

"But I don't like it when somebody comes and begs from me. It makes me feel--I don't know--all icky inside."

"Come on," says Dickie. "You just say, to yourself, 'There, but for the grace of God...' and hand over a quarter or something. A quarter buys a lot of wine."

"But doesn't it bother you?"

Dickie things. "I don't know. Maybe if I knew the person... but I can't imagine really knowing anyone who'd..." He fakes a shambling walk and gets a lot of laughs. Richard feels himself the newspaperman par excellance--but he's gotten into a couple of sticky things that make him wonder if he isn't putting out more than he wants to...he's bothered by ethical things--he's printed a story about a young man, member of city council, caught propositioning little boys. It's clearly a case of the public's right to know about its elected officials, and yet Richard knows he's ruined the man. The story hit the papers that morning. He's collecting all kinds of compliments on the writing of it--he's gone to the parents of the kids and gotten their feelings and really nailed the guy. He's spent today drinking in his room, trying to blot out what he imagines the guy is doing, but he's apprehensive---is it going to be worse if the guy manages to retaliate, or if he doesn't. He wants to talk about it, but Dickie is being the good host, which means not sticking around and talking to anybody about anything serious. Keep it light. The wives are talking diapers on one side of the room, the husbands are talking football on the other.

Then they play the stupid game. Line everybody up and shake around the house. The first one in line kisses the next and so on-- line's long enough so you can't see anybody. Dickie finds himself face to face with the Pope. Asks what to do, but the Pope won't answer. Then Richard gets to the end of the line and gets his slap in the face. "Lasagne!" Minniemouse announces gaily.

It struck Dickie as funny, as all strange things are a little funny, and so he'd grin a little whenever anybody asked. "Yes," he'd answer, "he never came back to work after that night. The girl at the switchboard tried calling his place all hours, but she never caught him home. Yes," he'd answer, "I never saw him again."

But Dickie would frown a little too, when he answered, for he was not telling the complete truth. He had seen Richard two or three times, before he'd stopped parking his car near the bridge, had seen Richard coming at him, or toward him, shambling along, wearing that apprehension less brilliant sweet smile one sees only on babies and drunks.

Three Presents

HE BULGING GROCERY BAG PRECEDED ANN LIKE A SECOND stomach as she waddled down her front walk to the waiting car. Three sets of English themes, two textbooks, seventeen student journals and a loosely wrapped tuna fish sandwich were crammed into the brown paper shell her arms embraced.

Inside the car, Lisa was confessing, "Each ball was $4.98. There's silk in the yarn." Ignoring Ann, Lisa was stroking the sleeve of her newest sweater, a lovely muted ivory, with rows of intricately knitted design and fashionably puffy sleeves.

Ann tried to decide which hand to knock with. Her right hand clutched the cloth handles of a library tote bag designed to carry five record albums; Ann had crammed in eight. Her handbag dangled from her left forefinger, unclasped and about to spill. She compromised by kicking Lisa's door.

It was probably less bad that Barbara was driving this morning. At least Barbara never honked her horn when Ann was late. Lisa muttered something angry as she threw open her door. Then, hunching forward toward the dashboard, she sighed an impatient, exaggerated sigh that let Ann know precisely how enormous an imposition she was making by entering last, and late, into Barbara's two-door Ford.

Afraid that the vibrations of her voice might explode her things, Ann motioned with her head toward the tricky latch at the base of Lisa's seat. Grudgingly, the other contorted herself, reached backward, and released the catch.

Ann tried to place her bundles neatly on the seat, but gravity seized them and they flew, open ends first, spewing papers. Headfirst, she followed her belongings.

Lisa was already engrossed in a complaint about one of her students, one of the many predictable features of her daily monologue. She seemed to have forgotten that Ann was there, or perhaps she was only underlining her annoyance when she pulled her door shut half in inch behind Ann's retreating heel. Yet there was a slight hesitation about today's chapter of Lisa Against The World, as if there was something else she might replace this with in mid-sentence.

And that was strange, for Lisa never hesitated. Lisa was perfect. Lisa was never late. She cooked; she sewed; she knitted; she worked full time. And she had two young sons, also perfect. At some point in each day's two-part talk, going to school or coming back, she managed to remind both Ann and Barbara of all these things.

Silently, Ann began retrieving her papers and books. On most days, by this time, she'd usually begun trying to pull the conversation into some area of more mutual interest, but today her mind was on the other thing.

Barbara glanced over her shoulder at Ann. "What happened today?" she asked. If Lisa had thought to ask that question, the tone would have been catty, and she would have put condemning emphasis on the last word to remind them again of her own perfection. But Ann and Barbara had been carpooling for years; Barbara could sense that it was time to be concerned.

Ann wondered if Barbara had noticed on her face the uneasiness and unexplained sense of loss that lingered in her mind. She slowed until she was piling up papers one at a time. She slowed because she did not know where she should start.

She guessed the first thing was the dandelions, which seemed to have appeared just this morning, the thousands of them, bright specks on her newly green back lawn. But it was not only the flowers; it was the picture of her little grey cat weaving among them, intent, it seemed to Ann, on nothing more sinister than causing no damage to each stem as she wound by.

If Lisa had not been there, she could have started with the flowers and the cat. Before Lisa pushed herself into their carpool last September, Ann and

Barbara had often talked about the changing of the seasons. But Lisa taught math; Lisa liked important facts. Particularly those facts about her own life that she was always inserting into any pause in conversation. For Ann, this was one more part of Lisa she would enjoy erasing; Lisa hated silence.

And she hated surprises in her schedule, hated being late. So Ann did not dare begin with the way that she had lingered over coffee on this warm spring day. She decided, instead, to begin with a lie, that she'd gotten a late start and was rushing to be outside on time for them.

And rushing, had not stopped to wonder why her cat was sounding muffled as she stood outside the back door, calling for Ann. Had not stopped to remember that May was the season of presents. Dandelions, scattered on lawns for kids to give their mothers. And other gifts that cats believed Nature had provided just for them.

The little grey cat had trotted in and dropped the bird just beyond Ann's shoe. Then the cat's head went up, and she began to fold herself in upon herself, smug as an Egyptian idol. The cat was absolutely still, looking up expectantly at Ann, a smile seeming to start from the white triangle beneath her nose.

The bird stirred. It tried one wing, then the other, then suddenly took off around the corner.

Forgetting time, Ann chased it into the tiled foyer, where the bird stopped to collect itself. It skidded on the tile and wobbled on its skinny legs. It shook its body, as if it had just finished a bath, then lifted its pronged feet one at a time. Then, having tested all its parts, it flew up and banked. Except that, having stopped against a baseboard, when it banked, it hit the wall.

Barbara's voice was breaking Ann's silence. The voice was worried, persistent. "What happened this morning?"

"Can I tell you...." It was Lisa, who could not let ten seconds go unfilled. Yet that same unfamiliar hesitation was in her voice. It was almost enough to tear Ann from her memories. Except that the image was so sharp before her eyes, as sharp as in a drawing: the sparrow banking, splaying out against what should have been thin air, but spreading itself, instead, against the yellow herringbone of her wallpaper and leaving four red spots. Then gathering itself again, half-freed from its confusion, and soaring parallel to the living room ceiling.

But then the picture window at the far end of the room confused it. Ann recalled the bump of bird against the glass as she wondered how to answer Barbara. For, vivid as the image was, it was not that picture that concerned her. That came later, or before--Ann did not know. And she did not want to think about it.

She grabbed at the bird with her open hand when it finally flew past her again. She had it in her fist before she realized what her hand had done. Her fingers closed on it as if she'd caught a ball, then untensed when she felt the warmth, the panicked breathing, the softness of the feathers and the fragile stoutness of the ribs. The bird's black eyes regarded Ann angrily, as if its problem was her fault. She took it out the front door and swatted it into the sky. The bird flew off at once, fairly steadily. In a second or two, Ann could not see it.

Ann turned back to the foyer, where the red spots snagged her conscience. And beneath the spots sat the cat.

For the little grey cat had followed her gift into the foyer and had settled herself again into the statue-position, expectant, almost smiling, waiting to be praised.

Instead, Ann began to harangue her for her cruelty, but before the lecture was halfway done, the grey head hung so low that the white triangle and the mouth seemed to have disappeared. The eyes were half-shut in shame. The attitude seemed familiar; that picture, not the picture of the bird, or of the spots, was the one that hurt, the one Ann could not date.

Then the mantel clock chimed seven, and Ann knew that she was very late.

Ann thought she knew now where to start, but Lisa, grown impatient, said again, "Can I tell you...." But this time she went on, in that special storyteller's chant she used when talking of her sons. Ann had often wondered if the tales were ever true. She would have sworn that Lisa polished them until the humor glistened, and then warned her listeners, "Can I tell you about this funny thing that happened...." There were tales of clothes discarded in undesireable public places, toys that wound up as snacks, babysitters frustrated into picturesque insanities. Lisa was starting off today's chapter with just the same four words. Yet today it did not flow smoothly.

Ann decided that the novelty was not great enough to keep her listening. Though Barbara, always polite, seemed riveted. Well, Barbara could listen for two; Lisa had never done anything but bore Ann before this. If she had wanted to deal with kindergarten problems, Ann thought, she would not be teaching high school. She wished that Lisa would hear her silences, and understand that they were hints.

But when Ann forced her mind to deal with other things, it kept returning to the four red spots. Then, swiftly, to the cat that sat beneath them, the cat with the downcast eyes. Something had happened this morning that saddened Ann far beyond the near-death of the bird, something that she could not quite recall. Or did not want to.

She turned again to Lisa's words. "...just checking on Brad before he went to sleep. And of course the piles in his room were Himalayan, maybe more than usual...."

Had she paused to collect their laughter, Ann wondered, or was this simply one more piece of Lisa's strange confusion.

"...but he kept looking at me, and then at the piles, like there was something....I could see a corner of a box sticking out from the biggest pile of all. Tell you the truth, I could make out the whole side."

Ann shifted in her seat, annoyed at Lisa for stringing this out so long.

"What it was...." Lisa said at last, "was this punchbowl. Brad and I saw it last weekend. One of your authentic Woolworth gems...."

The cat's face and the bird in its smiling mouth. And Ann remembered the shepherd and the sheep.

How old had she been? Probably Brad's age, whatever that was. She knew her numbers, but she still could not read words.

It hadn't been Woolworth's, but a store like it, and she had been looking for a long time, hampered by having saved only a dollar. The toaster that she'd found cost more than eight dollars. She'd found a housecoat without a price tag, but she did not know her mother's size.

And then she'd seen the massive statute on the counter, level with her nose.

"....where he got the money. It wasn't cheap. But that's not the point, not what I wanted to tell you."

The bright colors had drawn her to that counter where everything was ninety-nine cents. The shepherd was in the center of the scene, in navy pants and a maroon coat. A scarf of brilliant scarlet waved in the invisible wind that blew around his neck. His hat was chartreuse and pointed. In its bright yellow headband was a neon pink feather. The shepherd carried a gilded staff in one hand, and in the other was a long, crooked horn, gold with brown stripes. His cheeks and lips were rose-red spots, and his eyes were a blue as deep as his trousers.

To Ann's eyes, the five sheep were even more splendid than the boy that they surrounded. Noodles of clay fleece covered their backs. And each sheep was an entirely different color from the last. Each sheep had very large eyes of bright piercing blue, not too exactly painted into place.

And all of this glory stood on a pedestal with a gilt inscription Ann could not read.

"....navy blue glass and then there's this gold rim and rose overtones on the concave parts, and green highlights all over it."

"Sound perfectly...um..." Barbara probed, glancing back at Ann, still silent.

"Garish. Ghastly. You didn't think I...." Lisa began to chuckle. "But that isn't all. It has twelve matching cups--I mean exactly matching. And a ladle. And a matching plate that goes underneath to catch the slops."

Ann's pain was just as fresh as it had been that afternoon, and coupled with it, pain for Brad. Lisa seemed to be waiting for a response from somewhere, though, so Ann asked, "Are you sure the statue's meant for you?"

"What's wrong, Ann?" Barbara started. "She didn't say...."

But Lisa waved away this break into her talk and answered, "I wish I weren't so sure. Tomorrow's birthday. Besides...." Her mouth turned down wryly. "I guess I sort of asked for it."

Now Barbara was laughing along with Lisa. "How did you manage that?" she asked.

Lisa made a face. "Blame it on my sense of humor. You see, Brad and I were shopping last week, and when I saw this thing, just sitting on the reject counter in all its glory, I must've said something like, 'Have you ever seen anything like that?' I mean, the tone was very clear. But I guess when you're only six...."

The saleslady put the statue into a flimsy paper bag and Ann carried it home. She held one hand on the bottom so the fleece wouldn't cut through and break the bag. Her other hand clutched the neck of the bag so tightly that the paper became damp and wrinkled. Because the statue was so bulky, she could not free a hand to ring their doorbell. Instead, she stood on the stoop and called and called.

Her mother's face looked puzzled and worried. Ann knew then that she must have been gone for a very long time. To patch things up, she handed over the bag that was too big to hide. For that day was, after all, her mother's birthday. Then Ann waited, smiling, for the bag to be opened and for the praise to begin.

"Is this for me?" her mother asked. Ann nodded. But all her mother said was, "Oh."

Remembering, Ann's head dropped and her eyes half-closed in shame. She shook herself awake. She had never met Brad, had no idea what he might look like. But she knew that she must save him from his mother's tongue. Her mind, still half-connected to the shepherd and the cat, did not form quite the words she meant them to. "You're very lucky Lisa," she found herself saying.

"I guess that's my whole problem."

Angry at the Lisa she thought she knew, Ann heard the words, but not the sadness in the tone, so she persisted, "I wasn't talking about right now, about whatever Brad might give you tomorrow. I meant, you must have been a lucky kid, to always choose the right things...."

"If she did, she was undoubtedly the only one in the history of the world." Barbara was smiling at her own memories. "I bought a punchbowl once myself. Only it was a sleeping plaster Mexican. It was huge, but I thought it would be perfect for our dining room table. It was the biggest thing I could get with the money I had. My mother made a fuss." She paused, and thought about the fuss, and smiled. "She put it right out on our front lawn and it stood there for years."

"Mine was deodorant pads." Lisa's head was cocked to one side, and the sarcastic grin she usually reserved for the follies of others was now turned against herself. "My father gave me two dollar bills and orders to buy my mother a present. I went to the drugstore and picked out the fanciest jar I could find. I mean, I couldn't read yet. What did I know?"

"Mine was a shepherd. A shepherd and five sheep. I thought they were beautiful."

"And your mother didn't."

Ann, preoccupied again with her memories, thought that the statement came from Barbara, and missed, again, Lisa's tone. She shrugged. "My mother took it out of the bag, and I'll bet she spent at least three seconds looking at it. And then she put it on top of our china cabinet. Which had one of those fake Chippendale fronts. And that more or less hid the statue." Because Barbara had just pulled into the parking lot, Ann began again to put her papers into a neat pile. "My mother's house was very childproof. No statues. Nothing we could break and get in trouble for. I guess I'd never noticed it till then."

"It bothers you."

At last the sadness and concern in Lisa's voice was coming through to Ann. "I guess that when she saw it, she only thought the same thing I'd think now." Ann was looking at Lisa, yet all she could see were the cat's face and the bird's black angry eyes. "There might be gifts nobody could possibly expect you to be happy with. And yet...." Ann's hands rearranged the textbooks. "Yet I remember that shepherd. And all those sheep. I remember them down to the smallest detail. Because I was so proud....Yes, it bothers me. A lot."

Lisa sighed. On her face was a sadness that Ann had never seen there. Suddenly, Ann realized that it was not a question Lisa had asked her about whether she was hurt; Lisa had already known the answer. And she hadn't told today's story to amuse them or distract them, or to fill in the silence. She'd told it because she cared about Brad, and hoped they could show her some way not to hurt him.

And perhaps all of her endless tales about her children were just her way of thinking of them when she had to let them go.

Barbara pulled into her parking space and shut off the motor. Lisa began to gather up her own papers. Then she began to chuckle again. "I'll bet she was insulted, at first, by those deodorant pads. But then she found a way around it. She praised the jar. You know, she kept that jar. It sat right in the middle of her dresser for years." Lisa's hands stopped neatening her things. She took a deep breath. "It isn't a punchbowl, really, is it?" she asked the others. "That's not really what it's all about, is it?"

She stopped and thought again, and said, "But there's another problem. I already own a punchbowl. Which I almost never use. So I guess Brad has never seen it. But if he ever found out...."

Lisa got out of the car, turned, reached down to release the seat latch. She held out her free hand to Ann. "Here, let me have your stuff while you climb out of there," she offered. She pointed to a spot beneath Ann's feet and warned, "Don't step on your sandwich."

Barbara was watching them. She seemed about to speak, to make the offer, but Ann got there first. "Well, I don't own a punchbowl," Ann told Lisa. "I could use one."

"It's only milkglass," Lisa told her. "A cheap thing. I picked it up at a rummage sale."

It was the old Lisa, back in force. But somehow Ann found that she was not upset. "Milkglass goes with anything," Ann responded, wrapping her arms around the full brown paper bag. "I'll take it off your hands."

The Substitute

TWO DAYS AFTER THE FUNERAL, BERNIE WENT FOR AN EVENING walk in the alley behind his mother's house. It beat sitting and staring at Marty stare at his mother.

Marty had a habit of getting a little hysterical sometimes. Always had, since the days when Bernie had used him as his personal punching bag. "Bernie, that's not Mom inside there!" the kid had all but shouted at him this afternoon. "She's been sitting like that since the funeral. Just sitting."

"It's not like she isn't eating anything," Bernie told him. "Don't upset yourself...."

"Don't upset myself! That's our mother!"

"Marty, stop the shouting. Sarah and Sam were married thirty-five years. Her whole life was him. Maybe you don't remember how it was? How she'd spend the morning cleaning the house for him and the afternoon cooking for him, and then sit and wait by the door for him to come home? Thirty-five years is a long time to be together. You have to give her more than a couple of days to get things straight."

"You can talk," Marty whined. "You'll take off for the end of the world in two days. And I'll get left with the problem an hour away from my door."

"California isn't the end of the world, kid. It's only three thousand miles. I can get here fast enough by plane if you ever need me." But Marty needed him right now. Bernie could see that written all over his face. And he wasn't ready to give himself up, like a nickel deposit, on his kid brother's happiness. So what he was doing, out in the alley, was looking for something to leave here in his place, something tangible, though Bernie didn't know what, exactly.

The alley, divided into little pieces by spiked iron fences, shadowed over by dirty brick house backs and cluttered with garbage cans, did not make the world's greatest hunting spot; however, he hadn't rented a car when he'd arrived, making the alley the best he could do without begging Marty for a ride.

Suddenly, Bernie heard a prolonged yowl, like the cry of a baby abandoned. It came from a garbage can just beside his leg. Bernie undid the lid and found himself staring into a pair of yellow eyes. A pink triangle emerged from the darkness of the can and wiggled slightly, then a white mouth fell open. "Eee-yout," it demanded, like a rusty gate. Bernie scooped the cat out by its belly. He could feel the ribs through its matted grey fur. Did it belong to somebody else? Probably it had. It was far too large to have been born here; it was about the size of his own Siamese at home, and that cat was a year old. Clearly, someone had thrown it away and closed the lid tightly. The cat could not possibly have just climbed in, jarring it closed.

So here it was, he told himself, his tangible object, his substitute, a little soiled but, like himself, alive.

When he brought it into the living room, Marty objected immediately. "Mom never liked pets," he said.

"Sarah never liked dogs," Bernie reminded him. "Nobody ever asked her about cats." To Marty's grumbling, Bernie added, "Give her a week. If it turns out she doesn't like the cat, you can just toss it back into the street."

There was a soft rustling in the room as their mother shifted in her chair. Bernie walked to her and put his arm around her shoulder. "Hey, Sarah, look what I brought you," he said, pointing at the cat, who was preening herself in the middle of the rug.

His mother said nothing.

Bernie squeezed her shoulder gently. "Won't you at least give me a thank-you?"

"You're a good boy, Bernie." They were the first words her sons had heard from her in three days.

Marty sighed. "Why should she have needed a dog? She already had a pet," he said, not bothering to lower his voice.

Bernie shot a killing look at the kid. Then he picked up the cat and brought her to Sarah's feet. At once, the animal began licking her paw, then rubbing the paw across the top of her head. "See, Sarah, it's even self-cleaning," Bernie joked.

The woman nodded vaguely, then announced into the dining room, "Sam, company's coming!"

"What?" Marty was startled.

"Sam says that when a cat washes herself like that, company's coming. She's right, of course."

"Who?" Bernie asked.

"Why, the cat," Sarah explained patiently. "And just like she says, here you are. Marty comes in from all the way across town, and Bernie's here from California. Sam! Stop fussing with that and come out and talk to your sons."

Marty stared at Bernie. "She's really in great shape. I gotta hand it to you," he hissed.

As kindly as he could, Bernie told her, "Sarah, Sam's really...you know...."

"Why don't you just come out and tell her the truth?" Marty demanded in his ear.

"Give her time, I said," Bernie shot back, grabbing Marty hard. "The cat made her say more words just now than she's said in days. Isn't that enough for you?"

"But how is she going to be able to look after a cat? She can't even look after herself," Marty pointed at his mother, who was staring again at the front door.

"Cats can make it on their own," Bernie more or less quoted from a book his son had shown him during the opening skirmishes in the boy's campaign to get the Siamese. "All cats need is food and a clean litter box. I'll arrange for the neighbor's kid to come in for the box, and Sarah can feed it. She's always been good at feeding things," Bernie smiled, patting his brother's stomach.

"But suppose the thing dies on her?"

"It's not like it was worth money. It's an alley cat, kid, not a show cat." Bernie stopped and sighed. "Marty, look, it'll keep her occupied, give her mind something to think about besides Sam. I promise you, it'll work."

"You'll hear from me fast if it doesn't," Marty told him, although even he didn't believe it.

Sarah was alone. She sat and watched the front door. The door's frame was mahogany. A pane of glass, beveled on all four edges, took up almost half of the door. The handle of the door was carved in a design of snakes and flowers. She spent many minutes following the path of the snakes as they wound in and out of the flowers. Beyond the door, beside the door, it was all darkness. And Sam was not coming through it. The old clock chimed five, chimed six. The train had never been so late. The house was very empty with only herself in it.

She looked toward her feet. Large yellow eyes were looking back. The door was there again, all snakes and reveled glass. Then, there was the weight of the cat in the valley of the dress between her knees. Without thinking, Sarah put her hand on the cat's back. It was soft and warm. The cat breathed and Sarah felt the movement beneath her fingers. She stroked the silk back from head to tail, again and again and again. Soon a noise began somewhere inside the animal.. It was like the soft snoring sound the children made in their sleep. The sound pleased her, so she stroked the animal over and over. At last, Sarah looked closely at the thing beneath her fingers. It was not the grey shadow it had seemed on the rug. She could see now that there were tan patches on its hind legs. Its tail was ringed in black, and a pure white patch, like spilled milk, ran from its mouth to its chest. Sarah did not know how long she sat, tracing the shadings and colorings with her forefinger, but after a while she decided that Sam must have stayed somewhere else for the night and she stopped waiting.

For many days--Sarah did not count them--she wandered around the house. Was the furniture dusty? She wasn't really sure. Had she eaten? She wasn't hungry now, so she guessed that she had. Intermittently, her contact with the world was the tiny circle of light which included only the cat. When the cat was in her lap, she knew that by its warmth and weight. But she was never really aware of how it had gotten there, only that it was there.

Several times Bernie called from California. When the phone was not answered the first time, he told himself that she was out for a walk. The second time, he pictured her in the bathroom, turning off the shower, running for a towel. But then uneasiness began to nag at him, and so he called Marty.

"I finally got a chance to see Mom today," Marty told him enthusiastically.

"You only just saw her today?"

Marty's warm feelings were withered by the ice in his brother's voice. "Bernie, I get busy too...." he began.

"Okay, forget it," Bernie snapped, cutting him off. "Is she okay? What did she say to you?"

Bernie's anxiousness surprised Marty. It made him feel a little superior to shoot back, "Don't upset yourself."

"What did she say?" Bernie insisted.

"Well, like I said, I only just saw her. Through her window."

"You what?"

Hoping to forestall the anger he could hear building, Marty threw in, "Hey, thanks for that cat."

"What brings this on?"

"Well, see, like I started to say, all I could do was look through the window. I rang the bell and all, but I guess Mom didn't feel like opening the door. But the cat--Bernie, the cat looks great! So I figure, she'll act like kind of a thermometer if Mom doesn't want to answer the door. I mean, if the cat looks healthy, then Mom must have her wits about her enough to...."

"Why did you only look through the window?" Bernie's voice was menacing. If he could do it, Marty thought, he'd send that voice right through the wire and wrap it around my throat. "Don't you have a key?" the voice demanded.

"Well, yes, sure, but Bernie, Mom's a grownup woman now. I mean, if she wants to be left alone...."

"Use it!"

50

"And besides, Bernie, I don't know how to...."

"Use it!"

"What?"

"Use that key. Get yourself in there. And don't ever do that again."

Marty knew the tone. It was the one that had always preceded a beating.

So Marty used his key the next time, and the next. The cat would run to meet him. His mother would be sitting in an armchair, watching the door, waiting, he thought, to see him. But it was as he had feared: she would say nothing. He'd go on and on about his work, about his apartment, about the girls he was dating. He'd allot himself an hour, but an hour turned out to be a very long time to sit and talk and get no answer. He did that three times and then, hearing nothing from Bernie, Marty cut his visits to thirty minutes.

One afternoon, Sarah found herself standing at the kitchen sink, peeling potatoes for their supper. She became aware that the yellow eyes were staring at the peeler in her hand. The cat inched forward and stopped, inched forward and stopped, all the while watching closely as the parings coiled from the blade. "Is that interesting?" she found herself asking the cat, who was by now curled up around the hot water faucet. "This is a potato. Po-ta-to. I'm peeling it for supper, if you don't mind." The cat cocked her head at the unfamiliar sound of Sarah's voice, and peered up inquiringly. "This is a major operation, peeling a potato?" she asked the cat. The animal stared and stared, but it would not leave her side. Sarah walked across the room, noticing on the way that the floor could use a waxing. She looked at the cupboard door. The handle was coming a little loose. It was the first time she'd seen the door in weeks. She got out a pot. "This is called a pot," she explained to the cat, who had jumped from the sink to the floor and was following her. Sarah walked back to the sink. "I'm filling the pot with water and I'm putting in the potatoes and I'm boiling them until they're soft. Then I'll mash them up with a little milk and butter. You want some?"

The cat took in her explanation. She hopped up onto the counter near the stove as Sarah put the pot on to boil. At a comfortable distance from the flame, the cat sat and contemplated the surface of the water as the bubbles rose and fell. Sarah found herself watching the bubbles with the cat. "So maybe it is a major operation. Maybe life is full of major operations, if you just watch out for them," Sarah told the cat.

Just then, the cat lept from the stove and went running to the dining room, where it sat beneath the telephone with its head cocked. She followed the cat and found that the phone was ringing. It was Bernie, calling from California. Bernie's obvious relief was something she couldn't understand.

"Hello, Sarah, nice to hear you talking."

"Of course I'm talking. When did I not talk? I've been practicing on the cat, just in case you called."

Bernie ran the first half of that sentence through his mind. Practicing on the cat? Yes, that was something he could understand. He'd found that the Siamese had an overwhelming interest in carpentry, could sit for hours listening to his lectures on woodworking. Cats, he told himself, were things that dumb Marty would never know a thing about, one more link between himself and Sarah. Bernie was so busy congratulating himself that he failed to evaluate the second half of the sentence.

But Sarah, for all her talking, would never smile.

Bernie was calling two or three times a month. He'd ask after her health, and the cat's, and she'd tell him they were both fine. She didn't smile, but how could Bernie be expected to know that over the telephone.

Marty, of course, could see it, and was nearly alarmed enough to call Bernie. But then he asked himself if most people smiled at least once in the course of half and hour, then agreed with himself that most people did not. Bernie, he decided, would call him ten kinds of fool.

One Friday, Marty called his mother to say that he'd like to stop out for the weekend. Sarah started a chicken roasting, rolled out some noodles, and hung them over her towel rack to dry. She aired Mary's bedroom and dusted and swept it. She worked mechanically; her mother had taught her long before how to be a good hostess. Still, she told the cat, who was watching her from the threshold of the room, it did seem slightly odd to be playing hostess to your own son.

Sarah smoothed the mattress cover on the bed and pulled on the bottom sheet. She caught the top sheet by two corners and shook it out above the bed. A cool wind flew out and brushed her face. Slowly the sheet settled onto the mattress. Smooth whiteness stretched away from her. But there, near the head of the bed, was a lump. How had a lump gotten onto her clean bed? She hadn't noticed such a lump in the mattress when she'd stretched the bottom sheet onto it. But then, she hadn't really been looking for a lump either, she chided herself. She touched the lump; it miaowed at her.

"All right for you!" she told the cat. And she shooed it off the bed. She smoothed the sheet down again, looking around the four corners of the room. There was no cat in sight. But as she shook the blanket across the bed, Sarah saw the cat dart beneath it.

Sarah lifted the blanket from the cat's head. The animal was sitting upright, with her tail curled about herself like a queen in her robes, her train spread beneath her. The regal dignity was absurd. The cat smiled at Sarah; she smiled at the cat.

She pushed the cat from the bed and shook the bedspread out over the blanket. It made a flowered wing floating down. The spread settled. Again the lump, seemingly appearing from nowhere, and in exactly the same spot. Sarah, who had always thought herself in perfect control of things, felt helpless. She looked at the flowered lump sitting perfectly still, trying to hide from her and not in any way succeeding. The cat looked so silly that Sarah began to laugh.

"And so then there she was, sitting and looking at me like she was saying, 'Something bothering you?'" Sarah rehearsed the line to tell to Marty, but Marty never came. For Marty had become preoccupied with the problems of a client, and then with a golf game, then a girl. By the time he'd shaken himself free of his various preoccupations, it was eleven o'clock Sunday night. He told himself he'd only said he might come. If his mother was worried, he told himself, she would have called.

Sarah shared the best parts of the chicken with the cat and froze the rest. "It's a good thing noodles keep," she observed. On Monday morning, she stripped Marty's bed, washed and ironed and sheets and aired the blankets. "He said next weekend, that's the problem. My hearing isn't so good anymore, you know," she told the cat, who was sitting in her lap, rubbing her muzzle against Sarah's cheek in agreement.

By Wednesday, Marty's courage returned and he called his mother. She told him about the cat and the bed and laughed again, with him. "So then I realized that you'd said you'd be here this weekend, of course."

"Of course," Marty laughed, glad to be let off the hook so easily.

But if Sarah was letting him off, Bernie was pouring it on. When they were kids, Bernie would go through spells when he'd ignore Marty entirely. But then he'd change around and get on Marty's back double, as if to make up for his neglect. And it was like that now. "Are you going over there often enough? Twice a month? Twice a month is like next to nothing!" Marty, who realized that, stayed silent. But he was never sure if Bernie really cared about their mother, or if it was just a new variation of his old habit of making life miserable for his younger brother.

For Marty was miserable whenever he went to see her. There was something in the air in that house, something vague but terrifying. In his twenty-five years, Marty had never felt so terrified. If Marty had been able to put his finger on it, he would have told Bernie, but whatever it was, he couldn't put it into words.

Maybe it was the fact that she never seemed to mourn their father's death, never acknowledged that he was gone. No, that was not something to complain about. That, if anything, was cause for rejoicing, he guessed.

Maybe it had to do with Sarah's very obvious affection for Bernie's cat. But that was ridiculous. That was exactly why Bernie had given her the cat. How could he say that to Bernie without being accused of whining?

And so Marty swallowed his fears and increased the frequency of his visits.

Then Bernie arrived from California on business. After all his meetings were over and the reunions with high school friends, after he'd taken an uncle to dinner, Bernie went with Marty to their mother's house. "Hi, Sarah, how's my cat?" he greeted her.

Sarah was smiling. "Fine, fine."

The cat rubbed itself along Marty's ankle. Marty jumped back as if she'd bitten him. The feeling, the feeling was here again, and he couldn't place it.

"So what's doing?" Bernie wanted to know of Sarah.

"Nothing much. The cat and I find things to do."

The words were a little vague, Marty thought, but he could see that Bernie was encouraged by the smile that went with them.

She fed them pot roast, Bernie's favorite, and tomatoes from her garden. "I staked the tomatoes this year," she told them a little defiantly.

"So what's the big deal?" Marty asked, teasing.

"Sam always says to let them go--you get more tomatoes that way. But they always get so dirty, I tell him. So rotten on the ground. So I figure, if he's going to stay away so often on business, I'm just going to do them like I want to."

"That's great, Sarah. Let me know who wins," said Bernie, pretending to be enthusiastic.

It's here, Marty thought to himself. Why can't Bernie listen to it? Panicky, he found himself unable to eat anything.

"Suddenly you don't like my cooking, Marty?"

Bernie turned to him and scowled, and so Marty forced himself to eat what his mother had put on his plate.

"I've got chocolate cake, too," Sarah announced when their plates were clean.

"Sam never liked dessert," Bernie reminisced idly. The cat had come to loaf on his lap, and he was scratching her belly with his forefinger, almost hypnotized by her purring.

"Since Sam's not home tonight, I decided to do what you boys like," she said, the defiance now clear in her tone.

"My God!" Marty exclaimed, but Bernie was too busy smiling at the cat.

Having finished his cake, Bernie excused himself, loosening his belt and announcing that he needed a walk. Marty tried to stop him, tried to urge him to stay behind to help. "To help what? With dishes? Why are you getting so hysterical over a few dirty dishes?" Bernie laughed.

So Marty was left with his mother, the cat, the dishes and his fears. Maybe, he told himself, he hadn't heard what he thought he had heard. Maybe there was another way of understanding what she had said.

His mother smiled at him. "What's wrong with you?" she asked, picking up a chocolate-smeared dish. Following her with more dishes, Marty was about to answer when the cat, beneath his feet, began to lick her paw and run it over the top of her head. "Company's coming, Sam!" she called out gaily. Then she stopped herself. "That's silly," she said, more to the cat than to Marty. "Sam isn't even home tonight."

Marty slammed the dishes onto the sink. "Mom, Pop isn't coming home tonight," he burst out. "He won't be coming home ever!"

Sarah looked bewildered. "What do you mean?" she asked, setting down the dish and reaching for the cat.

"Pop's dead, Mom. We buried him months ago. You remember that, Mom. Mom, you have to remember!"

Sarah shook her head. "How can I remember a thing that never happened?"

Marty felt the thing all around himself. "Mom, it happened. Somehow your mind had missed it, but it happened. You have to believe it!"

"Sam's away on a business trip. That happens."

"Mom, you can't go on like this."

"If it happened like you say, why didn't Bernie ever say anything like this to me? Why didn't Bernie ever mention it before?"

"Mom, I don't...."

"No, Marty, you're wrong. Of course, I can go on like this," Sarah said very calmly. "I'm happy. I'm healthy. What do you want from my life?"

Bernie had come in on the last question. "Marty, lay off her," he commanded. He seized Marty's shoulder as if he wanted to wrench it off.

"Mom, please, tell Bernie what you just told me," Marty begged. "Bernie, you lay off me for once and listen to what's going on here."

But his mother was busy rubbing her face against the cat's face as Bernie threw a protective arm around her.

Late one afternoon, Sarah was sitting in the chair waiting for Sam to come home from work. The late sunlight was making the gold in the watered-silk paper sparkle. Sarah looked around her at the pictures on the wall, at the grey velvet sofa, the armchairs and marble-topped tables. She peered into the dining room at the dark oak table and chairs and sideboard. "Tomorrow, we have to get that dusted," she told the cat, who was sitting on her lap. She began to run her hand down the animal's back. The cat rubbed its face against hers rhythmically, sinking its claws into the thick web of her sweater. First she rubbed one side of her face against Sarah's, then the other, until Sarah was forced to turn her full attention to the animal. Sarah began to talk to the cat softly, stroking her from the top of her head to the tip of her tail. The yellow eyes widened and glowed green in the afternoon sunlight. "Sweet cat," Sarah crooned, as she had once crooned to Bernie, then to Marty.

Suddenly, carried away by affection, the cat nipped Sarah on the chin. Sarah cried out and struck the cat, pushing her away. The cat ran off and cowered motionless in the dark shadows beneath the dining room table. Sarah was startled, but she was unable to rise. Instead she remained in the chair and turned from side to side, looking frantically as far as the dim twilight allowed. But Sarah could not find the cat in the gloom. She buried her head in her hands and sobbed for the loss of the cat.

She sobbed as she had not sobbed before, having never, as far as she could recall, lost anything so precious. What had Marty tried to tell her? That Sam was gone? That he was lost in the darkness? Gone as the cat was gone? She cried until her eyes burned, until her hands were wet with crying. And she moaned aloud, over and over again. The cat, hearing this sound she could not identify, came out of the darkness and sat at Sarah's feet, head cocked, listening. The yellow eyes glinted, and after a long time of sobbing, Sarah raised her head and saw them.

"Oh," she said. "Oh, I thought I had lost you, but here you came back." She tapped her thigh, their signal for the cat to come again. "There was no reason for you to run away. No reason for you to go. Nobody goes a way for good when there's no reason to go. Nobody," she told the air defiantly.

The cat looked at her and seemed about to speak. But she was only gauging the distance between the floor where she had crouched and Sarah's lap. Wordless, she sprang, then began nuzzling Sarah's cheek once more.

Sarah was watching the door long after the streetlight went on and caught the snakes and flowers in its beam.

the end

Ruins

BY NOON, THE LINES OF TOURISTS AT THE WATER FOUNTAINS were spilling onto the blacktopped parking lot. Tourist families packed the small grocery store and cafeteria near the museum, and seized the round tables embedded in concrete on the patio beside the store.

In the grove on the other side of the museum, the picnic tables had all been filled. The man and woman from Milwaukee had just spread their sandwiches proprietarily on a table, when a dusty red Volkswagen, seven or eight years old, pulled onto the grass at the edge of the site. Camping gear filled the back seat of the small car, and tent poles, like broken bones, protruded from the tarpaulin that covered the luggage rack. Two loosely rolled sleeping bags threatened to unwind themselves and escape from beneath the gray canvas.

The young driver detached himself from the vinyl seat. He wore heavy hiking boots, faded denim shorts, a torn Navy dungaree work shirt, open to the waist, and a three-day-old beard. Smiling, he started toward the table, but tripped over the metal chain that secured it to the nearest tree. "Jesus H. Christ!" he said bitterly.

The older man stared at him.

"Listen," the young man said, "all the tables are full. There have to be two dozen screaming brats at every one. Can we sit here?"

The others said nothing. The man began to tear crumbs from a corner of his sandwich.

"Look, we're reputable. I'm Princeton, '72. The lady in the car is majoring in philosophy."

The older man shook his head negatively.

"Goddammit," the young man continued, "we drove all morning. Started out from Ouray at seven, drove those damn mountain roads in this heat, fifteen miles an hour. We got behind some asshole dragging a trailer. Car had a gear halfway between my first and second, and I had to keep shifting back and forth, so I wouldn't drive right up his ass. When we finally spotted the mesa, we decided to take a quick look up here before we went to the campground, but now that we've arrived, we suddenly feel all broken down. We had to get out of the car and get something cold to drink. And then we discovered that all the damn tables were overrun. Except yours."

The older man was about to refuse him, when a young woman popped from the car. A peasant bandanna kept her long straight hair from falling into her face, and her denim skirt looked freshly pressed. "I was being ridiculous," she said, "and I was too frightened to do any of the driving through those mountains. I wouldn't even drive on the roads up here. George and I crossed the Colorado line two weeks ago, and he's been doing the driving since then. It was cool, though, until we started south from Ouray. Then the heat got to both of us."

The older woman looked slightly less grim. The girl pressed her advantage. "It was foolish of us to buy a foreign car. It's much too small. The previous owner was a friend, and yet I'm not sure I trust it to get us home again. What do you think?" She came to the table, avoiding the chain, and sat down on the end of a bench.

Without a word, the older man moved toward one end of the table and indicated that the young man and his woman could stay. The young man took a knapsack from the back of the car and threw it onto the table. "It is so damn hot here," he said. "Is there any place a person can get something cold to drink?"

"There's a pop machine outside the men's john," the older man said. "Lucky for you, you stopped by us. We only just saw it on the way back from the store. When we first got up here, there wasn't nobody that looked like you could trust them, so we drove all the way up past the museum and bought some Cokes. Cooler's back at our trailer, and the stuff was warm by the time we got back and grabbed this last table. Come on, I'll show you."

After the two men had gone, the women sat silently. All around them, children were shrieking. A Greyhound bus pulled up across the road. The driver stepped down and looked at the filled tables. Then, opening the luggage compartment, he pulled five styrofoam coolers onto the ground. Two dozen teenagers stepped out and arranged themselves on the ground around the coolers. The driver handed out sandwiches and cans of soda. After a few minutes, he took three watermelons from the coolers and cut them into large slices with a long knife. He wiped his juice-wet hands on his trousers and handed around the melon chunks. There were many pieces left after everyone had been served. A boy and a girl took the blue cooler lid and piled on the Christmas-colored pieces. Then they held the lid between them and, laughing and shouting to the others on the ground, strolled from one picnic table to the next, distributing the fruit. When they reached the pair of women, they held out their tray. Smiling, the younger woman took pieces for herself and her companion. Water crystallized on the melon and glittered in the hot sun. Turing to the older woman, the other said, "Would you like a piece for yourself and your husband?"

The grim expression settled again on the older woman's face, and she waved her had at the teenagers as if she were swatting biting flies. They backed away in silence, and went on to the next table. "You ain't really going to eat that," the older woman said. It was a statement, not a question.

"Why not?"

"You don't even know them people. Don't you read in the paper, how kids get killed from free Halloween candy, and like that?"

The girl burst out, "But we saw them eating...." Then she stopped herself and said, as if continuing the same conversation, "My name is Jean. You never told me yours."

Then they heard the two men returning. "Hey, guess what?" the older man shouted at them, "he says he wouldn't sleep without a tent on a bet!"

"Is that important?" Jean asked.

"Well, you see, there was these Mexicans sleeping out at the campground last night. They didn't have no tents or nothing. They come up in a big flatbed truck, and I guess they spread their blankets in back of the truck and slept out in the open. We got up about six a. m., trying to beat the heat on the Cliff Palace tour, and we saw them on our way out. I says to the wife, 'Who knows what all they done in plain view last night?'" He winked at his wife and laughed. "The grownup ones was passing around this one can of juice, and everybody was drinking right from the can, one after the other. The kids was getting dressed right in front of everybody."

"I wish we didn't need a tent," Jean said softly. "I wish we were familiar with the weather here, and could trust it that much."

They all sat down and began to eat in silence. Suddenly the older man put down his soda can. "I bet you thought, when you saw us sitting here, that we was staying at that fancy new motel near the information building. But that ain't so, you know. We got a trailer back at the campground. They don't let you tow it all the way up here." He took a sip of his soda. "Say, how'd you like to follow us back and take a look at our place? Besides, you better get a campsite before they're all taken."

"Aren't you staying to see the museum?" Jean asked.

"No, the heat's got to us too. We just decided to go home and take a nap when you came up."

"I guess we'd better get a site," Jean said. "We can see the museum later."

"Groovy," said the young man, almost under his breath.

At the campground, the older man pulled in beside a massive porcelainized aluminum trailer. It was a VueKleer Explorer. "You can wash off anything you pick up on the road," its owner explained. Five stickers decorated the back end. "There's New Mexico," he said, pointing at a sleeping four color Mexican. "We went there before we came up here. We was at Durango day before yesterday," he continued, picking out a two-inch-high steam locomotive that seemed to be steaming directly at his finger. He unlocked his door and the others followed him inside. He locked the door again behind them.

"I miss my peekhole," his wife complained.

"We got a peekhole in the front door at home," he explained for her. "Lets you get a look at who's outside. You got the upper hand then, you know?"

Jean stepped to a small formica topped table and sat down. "What a lovely kitchen you have," she said to the older woman.

"We like it. I got a stove and oven, and this here under the sink is the icebox. It's small, but it's handy."

"All we have is a two-burner Coleman stove," Jean said. "I heat the water for the dishes while we eat, and then I wash the dishes in a pan we carry in the camp kitchen. Which is just a fancy name for a big wooden box. It's not handy at all."

The two women laughed.

"There's a double bed goes over the table, when you shove it down. This seat makes up into a single bed, and that couch across the front folds out," the older man said.

"Seems like a lot of beds for the two of you," the young man observed. "You must do a lot of sleeping."

"Yeah. Well, we got this one son at home yet. He didn't come along on this trip."

"Oh?"

"We got into this fight the Sunday before we left. Asked him to go to church with us, that's all I did. But he says, why should he go to church to learn what Hell is when he knows what it is, just by living in America. Whatever he means by that...It's a shame, too. We just bought this thing this year, bought it, partly anyways, so he'd come with us. Thought it might...I don't know. Would you've gone if your parents had a thing like this one?"

There was a silence.

Jean broke in again, "I like the decorating you've done, the curtains and flowers. Our tent can get to looking bare after a while."

Another silence.

Finally, the older woman responded, "You need something to make it look like home." She paused. "Not that home is such a great place anymore. Now, my sister lives in a part of town where they put in these new street lights. The pink ones?"

"Lights up the whole neighborhood, front, back and sides," her husband put in.

"Nice, right?" the other man observed with a wry smile. "I'll bet there hasn't been a kid who's been able to see the stars for months."

"I bet you can't see the stars inside that tent of yours neither," the older man snapped. "The point is, like your wife says, it's good protection."

"Have many people been beaten up?" Jean asked.

"Less than there used to be, when there wasn't these lights. You know, the world don't have to be such a bad place, if you do something about protecting yourself."

"Like the lights?"

"Yeah. And like, there was all these bus drivers got beat up. People stole the money they kept to make change with. So now you just have the right fare or they give you a slip and you go down to the bus company and get your change back."

"It brings people together," his wife added. "I was sitting on the bus the other day. This young man got on, and he only had a dollar bill, and so he had to ask around to find somebody with change. It's the first time I saw people talking to one another on the bus in, oh, I bet a year!"

The younger man leaned back against a closet. "But do you really have to go all the way to the bus company to get your money back?"

"I guess you could get it by mail," the older man conceded, "if somebody didn't grab it before you got to it."

"How many robberies had there been before this new system was introduced?"

"Enough."

Jean broke in again. "It's so hot here. Did you notice all the people waiting for water near the restrooms?"

There was a silence, then the older man said, "Hey! I bet you could use a cold beer."

"That would be wonderful," Jean said.

"Groovy," the young man observed morosely.

"I like it here a lot." the older woman said.

Her husband closed the icebox door and straightened up. He took four juice glasses from the cupboard above the sink and divided two cans of beer among them. "There ain't so much to worry about," he agreed. "A person can walk around, even leave his car open, so long as there's nothing worth taking in it. We been leaving everything locked in the trailer. We bought a cooler to save money, but then we found out you can buy pop cheap enough just about anywhere, so we started leaving the cooler behind. That way, we get to leave the car windows down and have some air."

Jean stood up and smoothed her skirt. "We really have to be going," she said. "Thank you so much for the beer."

The older man unlocked the door. "Comes over again," he said. "We'll be here till Thursday."

When the young people were outside again, they heard the door behind locked.

He lay in bed for nearly two hours, but the heat would not let him sleep. His wife sighed and turned, but seemed to be dozing, so he rose and left the trailer. He drove out of the campground and wound his way up the mesa, past the museum, looking for something they would not want to see together. Ahead, where the road widened briefly to three lanes, he saw a brown sign which announced that three quarters of a mile away, by foot, there was a lookout.

He parked the car in the third lane and started down the dusty orange-brown path. There was no one else, no cars and sounds. At first, he was striding briskly up the path, letting the dust grey brush hit against his pants and fall away, listening to the slight rattling scuffle of the small leathery lizards as they ran away from him, and then to the unbroken silence. There wasn't a bird in sight, not in the sky, not in the black, leafless trees scattered along the path. But suddenly he slowed, thirsty and hot and a little dizzy. He felt that there was something peculiar about this heat, and when he sorted it out, he realized that the sun was doing its work so efficiently that the moisture of his body was not being given time to collect on his skin in pools; the sun was stealing it from him without even letting him sweat. And without sweat, his Midwest-conditioned body had not been able to warn him that it was probably too hot for him to be walking like this.

He leaned against one of the trees. It was barely taller than he was, black and dry. It seemed almost dead, except for one half of one branch which still had some green leaves on it. The bark was very rough against his skin. A short way ahead of him, a hand, now long gone, had arranged a line of stones to point the way along the path to the lookout. Suddenly, the brown-orange dirt showing everywhere through the dry brush, reminded him of the scalp of his grandmother showing itself through her scant hair. She had been almost dead on the day he was remembering, and by now had been dead and rotting forty years.

Again he became aware of the complete silence, of the terrible drying heat of the sun. He judged that he was more than halfway to the lookout by now, and decided to try the rest. The road bent and slanted downward to the edge of a high bluff. In his dizziness, he felt that he would keep walking downward until he walked off, without being able to stop. But as he approached the edge, he saw that a steel pipe guard rail formed a boundary, and against the rail stood the young man from the picnic ground, who was peering through a pair of binoculars at the cliffs across the canyon floor. As the older man staggered down to the rail, the young man lowered the glasses and held them out. "Look for the black spots," he said. "It's the only way you'll ever find them."

The sun burned on the two men. "Find what?" the older man asked, wetting his lips with his thick tongue.

The younger man saw the motion, and saw that the man had no canteen. He held out his own. "Have a drink," he said, "and then I'll tell you."

The older man took the canteen, wiped off the lip carefully, then took three long swallows of the warm, metallic water. Then he replaced the cover, and the young man took it back. "Hold this open," the young man directed, stepping to a metal box on a pedestal rooted to the concrete.

The older man mechanically lifted the lid and held it. Inside the box was a photograph of the cliffs directly opposite them. Superimposed on the picture were numbers, and below the picture was a key which told how many rooms, for how many people, had been constructed in the crevices of the rock. Beyond the area represented on the picture, the cliffs stretched for miles in either direction. "Look for the slack spots," the young man directed again. "They're the windows and doors." He handed the older man the binoculars. "Did you get to the museum yet?" he asked.

"We were saving that till tomorrow. We were supposed to do it this afternoon, but the wife conked out for good after you left."

"Then let me tell you about it. It's quite a place. You see, these people lived on the top of the mesa for hundreds of years. They were farmers, and they traded with other Indians from all over the area. First they dug holes in the ground, with roofs on top. Then, some years later, their houses became more elaborate, but they always retained a room in the ground as a ceremonial room, a church of sorts." He paused and smiled at the notion. "Shortly before they moved to these...places...they were building whole villages, and there'd be one of these kivas in every village.

"But then something happened. And the really insane thing is that the archaeologists can't decide what it was. But whatever it was, it forced them to move into the cracks in the cliffs, the same cliffs their cave-dwelling ancestors had hidden in thousands of years before. But by now, of course, they had become builders, and so they dragged stones up those sheer cliffs from the valley floor, and used them as bricks to build their houses within the crevices. In the largest crevices there are whole cities, with apartment buildings that rise several stories. And for every apartment house, they built a kiva."

"Yeah, we saw that at the Cliff Palace."

The young man paused again, opened his canteen, and drank. "You know, before we came out here, I pictured these cliff dwellings as being on the outside walls of the mesa, looking out over that beautiful endless expanse of land, the way the information building does. But they're all in here, in this narrow canyon, buried down here in the middle of the mesa, and how far would you say you can see? A mile across? A few miles, side to side? I'll bet that in some of those smaller crevices across from us, where you can't stand up, and where there's no rock ledge in front of you, you can't even see as far up as the sky!"

The two men stared at the miles of yellow cliffs and the sharp forbidding talus that fell to the canyon floor. "I'll admit," the young man continued, "that some of the larger apartment houses aren't so bad. There's breathing room, at least. In the Balcony House, there seems to be a court where their kids must have played, and there's a brick wall to keep them from falling and cracking their skulls on the talus. And then there's the entry. Did you read about the entry?"

"We went to the Cliff Palace this morning, like I said before, but we saved the rest for later."

"Well, there are two huge boulders that stand against the face of the cliff. The Indians found that between the boulders and the cliff there were crevices wider than a man, and between the boulders was a kind of natural room. The cliff-dwellers carried stones up the face of the cliff and walled up the sides of the crevices until only one man at a time could pass through. They also bricked up the top of the crevices, so that anyone coming or going would have to crawl on his hands and knees. But they left the chamber, so that a man could stand up and rest between crawls. Now, when someone would come crawling out of the entrance, a resident would be waiting for him with an upraised club. If the newcomer was a friend, then he was allowed in. But if he turned out to be an enemy, he'd get it over the head, before he had a chance to stand up. Nice, right?"

The older man was still scanning the cliffs. He shrugged and said nothing.

"It's so damn hot here," the younger man continued. "And some of these 'homes'" he said, his lips twisting around the word, "are a mile and a half from the nearest spring. And of course they couldn't have ladders, because an enemy could use a ladder too, so there are just toeholds in the rock. Have you tried doing anything strenuous at this altitude?"

He paused. The other, realizing an answer was expected, said, "Yes, it's rough."

"Damn straight! Can you imagine carrying one of those big pottery pitchers a mile and a half to the spring, and then back, full of water, straight up those cliffs? I mean, I have trouble hauling a full plastic jug." He took back his binoculars and scanned the rock walls. "And those little ones in the crevices over there. Some of them aren't four feet high. And the windows were shaped so that a stone could be pulled into them and no enemy could tell, from where we're standing, that the rooms were there at all."

"Pretty clever for Indians, I mean, that early on."

"Clever? Jesus! Can you imagine hiding in one of those, not being able to stand. Not being able to see, except for a little light coming in around the edges of the stone. Staying there, perhaps for days, scared, with no water, virtually no air, in this heat? What were they so afraid of? What could possibly have been so bad, to make them get off the top of the mesa and come down to this?"

The older man shrugged again and walked to another corner of the pipe fence. The younger man followed him, letting the cover of the box clang shut. "And for what? The irony of the place is that with all those precautions, they still disappeared."

"Disappeared?"

"Yeah, within a hundred years of the time they came off the top of the mesa. They just vanished, evaporated. The archaeologists can't find a trace of warfare, or of disease. Nothing."

The wind picked up and came whistling at them down the canyon. Nearby, five turkey vultures appeared out of nowhere and began to soar in a circle, silently and slowly.

Encouraged by what seemed a promise of coming coolness in the wind, the older man turned and started up the path. The younger man came after him, binoculars bouncing against his chest.

"Where's your wife?" the first called back over his shoulder.

"She dropped me off and went back to shop for souvenirs."

"What gets me," the older man confided over his shoulder, "what really gets to me about this place is...well, we got this model of the park in our museum at home and, I swear to God, this looks just like it."

Goat

HE MOHEL WAS DRUNK UPON ARRIVAL AT HIS CIRCUMCISION, and from that day on, bad luck followed Shlomo.

His only brother left for America on Shlomo's twentieth birthday. Two weeks later, Shlomo's village was burned and his parents with it.

Shlomo was the only survivor.

He travelled to Kiev, looking for work, and found employment hauling ashes. He had a dog, but the dog died. He had a wife, but the wife died too. Having no more, he wrapped his extra shirt about his father's watch and booked passage to Boston.

Boston was noisy, dirty and crowded. When he inquired after his brother, he was told that the older boy had long before gone to Philadelphia. Shlomo hauled ashes for three weeks, purchased a train ticket, and went on.

Shlomo stood on the train platform with his bundle in his arms. He looked to his right and saw, between the backs of rushing people, a flight of grey steps and a littered platform. He looked to his left, but there were only more steps, more litter. He began to walk. The hollow sound of his own feet followed a second behind him. He stopped; the sound stopped. He began again; the sound, lonely and frightening, began behind him.

Near the steps stood an older man. "You're looking for someone?" he asked.

Shlomo shook his head and shrugged. The man looked at his hat, his face, his coat, pants and shoes. "You're looking for someone?" he said in Yiddish.

Shlomo smiled. "You know my brother, Aaron Jacobs?"

"No...."

"They said he was in Philadelphia."

"It's a big city."

"But without him I have no place to stay."

The other's eyes widened. He struck a pose, with finger to his lips. "I tell you--I was here looking for a sister, but she never came. At my place is a couch--five dollars a week."

"But I don't..."

"Wait, wait, when you find work, five dollars....My wife makes wonderful soup--with matzo balls."

Shlomo frowned.

"I'll throw it in free for nothing."

He put his arm around Shlomo's shoulders. "My name is Mendel. I run a junk shop on South Street....old magazines, metal goods, clothes, books..."

"Shlomo Jacobs."

"From?"

"Kieva Gubernia."

"A coincidence! A landsman!"

"You're from Kiev?"

"Near, near."

They climbed the stairs to the sun. "So you'll stay?"

Shlomo nodded.

Within a month, Shlomo had found a house and a job.

The house was a shack, abandoned by the construction crew of a project which was only half-completed when funds ran out. It was by the river. The cold wind whined through the cracks in the wooden walls in winter, and the smell of the city's garbage filled the single room in summer. But it kept off most of the rain, and cost nothing.

The job occupied him ten hours a day, every day of the week save the Sabbath. It brought him two miles across the city to a large pottery. There Shlomo spent the daylight hours sweeping pottery dust, collecting broken crockery, carting all stacks of plates and cups from one floor of the pottery to another, and hauling ashes. After his work day ended, Shlomo walked back across the city, down South Street, across Second, to his shack. Most evenings, he was too tired to make a meal, but sat outside, watching the stars, the new bridge, and the garbage scows.

He rarely had visitors, for his home was almost a mile from the tenements of South Street where the landslite lived. Only on Saturday mornings did he meet the rest, at synagogue, when they all gathered for a bit of wine and cake after the service. He would stand against the wall, holding his plate of cake and looking. He saw them all, and knew them, although they did not know him.

Mendel came to him regularly. The first time, he brought a stack of month-old Yiddish newspapers. Shlomo broke down and in a rush came the story of his lost parents, the brother, the village and Boston. In the weeks afterward, Mendel came bearing bargains from his shop, and Shlomo bought him out. So Shlomo lived, alone, unknown, in his cold shack--to work six days a week and rest on the seventh, as it is written.

It was five years later, on a May morning, that Shlomo heard a word, a rumor, of his brother. It was said that the brother was a prosperous businessman in Frankford.

Shlomo went to Mendel and together they went to the Montreal. Mendel put Shlomo on the first car with written instructions. He stood and waved as the train pulled away.

Shlomo rode for a full hour, three stories above the street, in a green and glass, wood-steel car that rattled and rocked down the track. He held the instructions in his hands and stared out the window at the brownstones and banks flying by. Shlomo got off the train when the conductor shouted "Last stop. Frankford!" as it said on the paper.

His brother's store was at the base of the stairs. The sign said, "Jacobs" as he had heard. But the interior was dark, the door bolted. Shlomo stood and looked at the sign.

A woman came from the bakery adjacent. "Jacobs' store will be open tomorrow."

"Tomorrow?"

"Well, aren't you impatient? After all, the funeral was only yesterday."

Shlomo walked, following the El tracks to the river and the river to the shack. He closed the door and did not come out until morning.

One morning that summer, when the temperature rose to a hundred and the humidity followed close behind, the owner of the pottery closed the shop for the day. Shlomo began to walk. He found himself at last at the entrance to the bridge which he had seen from his shack. He walked across. A sign welcomed him to Camden, but he hardly noticed it. He walked silently on. Shortly, he passed the limits of the city and found himself at the gate of a farm.

There was a scattering of animals in the farmyard. Twelve white chickens buried their heads in the sand. As Shlomo watched, a large uncombed dog ran through them. They broke apart, but settled soon in the sand a few feet away.

And then, a young goat limped out of the barn and came to the gate. Shlomo put his hand hand through the bars. The goat came to him and put her head against his hand.

Suddenly a voice, "What do you want here?"

The farmer walked toward him from the house. Shlomo said nothing.

"I said what do you want?"

The goat rubbed her head against Shlomo's pants.

"You want to buy the goat? She's not much good. Lame. I got others."

Shlomo shook his head.

"One dollar."

Shlomo took a dollar from his pants. The farmer pocketed it quickly and shooed the goat through the fence. Shlomo began to walk back toward the city. The goat followed.

They walked through the countryside. For the first time Shlomo noticed the flowers in the yards, the tomato plants in rows, the cabbages, the onions, the stubby green pines. And the goat limped behind him.

They walked through the streets of Camden, across the bridge, and down Fourth Street to South. Down South Street they went,

Shlomo and his goat, down the narrow street, hemmed on both sides by high brown buildings. Around the tables, piled with clothing they went, ducking the dresses which hung in place of awnings on the pipe-skeleton frames. Past the piles of potatoes, carrots and beets in tilted wooden crates they went, under the low-hanging store-front marquees. Harry the Shill from Gold's Superior Clothing Emporium hooked his cane into Shlomo's collar and began to drag him into the store; but when he saw whom he had snagged, he smiled and shrugged and waved him on.

Shlomo and the goat passed between the tables of twine and balls and bottles and entered Mendel's shop.

Mendel came from behind the glass counter. The goat stopped beside Shlomo. Mendel looked at the goat. "What have you got there, my friend?" He rubbed the goat's ears.

"I bought her."

"What then, you stole her?"

Shlomo smiled.

"Where did you get her?"

"From a farmer."

"She gives milk?"

"I didn't ask."

"It is a she?"

"I guess so."

"You didn't look?"

Shlomo had no answer.

"But for what did you buy her?"

"To keep."

"No, Shlomo, not to keep. Look, you live alone in that shack, they don't bother you. They figure, one man, so who's he hurting? But when they see the goat there too, they figure, a rich man--he can afford to buy a goat! Why does he need the shack? They throw you out, next thing you know."

"You think so?"

"I know so!"

Shlomo turned and began to walk out. The goat followed.

"Wait a minute, wait a minute. We'll figure something out."

73

Shlomo stopped and the goat stopped behind him.

Mendel pursed his lips and stared at the ceiling. "Ah hah!" he said finally.

"You thought of something?"

"Of course, I thought of something. Leave it to Mendel to think of something! We'll have a lottery."

"A lottery?"

"It's the very thing."

"Somebody else would want the goat?"

"A beautiful animal like that? Who gives three quarts of milk a day?"

"Three quarts?"

"At least!"

"They would make me move out of my house?"

"Absolutely!"

Shlomo thought. He looked at the goat. He bent down and rubbed behind her ears. "But how will we let people know?" he asked.

"A sign in a couple windows. A word here and there. My good friend, you take your goat home. Keep her in the house. If somebody says to you 'Mendel sent me' you'll know he's a customer and you show him the goat."

"You're sure I'll have to move?"

Mendel sighed. "Shlomo, my dear Shlomo, it's such a good business deal. Look, how much did you say you paid for the goat?"

"A dollar."

"A dollar. We charge, say, twenty-five cents a chance. We sell fifty, sixty chances. I take a little off for commission. You figure a little off for food. And you make, let's see, ten dollars."

Shlomo turned toward the door.

"That's ten dollars minimum!" Mendel called after him.

"No, that's all right. You go ahead and make your plans."

It began the following morning with Hinda Cohen, wife of the largest wholesaler in the area. She came at eight. Shlomo was watching a freighter being pulled from its moorings.

"Hello, Shlomo!" Hinda called.

"Did Mendel send you?"

"Well, I was coming by this way on my way to shopping and I thought I would drop in and see you."

Shlomo said nothing.

"I thought you might like a little company." Hinda took a step forward.

"I can't let you in unless Mendel sent you."

"Well, now that you mention it, Mendel did say something about a little...business deal you two were planning."

"Yes..."

"I mean, it's not as if I needed the goat...but my children might like to have a pet, I thought, and we have a big house to keep her in, and Mendel said she gives milk too."

"You want to see the goat?"

"Well, if it's not too much bother..."

The goat was standing in the corner of the shack. Hinda squinted, inspected under and over, ran her hand down the goat's back, squatted down and looked at the udder, then stood back to get a picture of the whole. "A quarter you want for that?"

Shlomo grew red, but said nothing.

"That Mendel! He must have talked you into this."

"I paid a dollar."

"Well, from such a goat I know I won't get much but trouble. But it says in the Yom Kippur prayers, 'charity.'"

She gave Shlomo a quarter. He took it and put it in his pocket. "My ticket," said Hinda, holding out her hand.

Shlomo took a slip of paper from the table, printed a figure one twice, and ripped the sheet in half. He gave one half to Hinda, and put one half in a bowl on the table, as Mendel had told him.

"Well, it was very nice talking to you," Hinda said. And before Shlomo returned to his seat, she had disappeared up Market Street.

So he sat, all morning long, enjoying his freedom, for Mendel had called the potter, his employer, and had begged off work in his name for the three days until the drawing. At intervals, he would enter the hut and scratch behind the goat's ears without a word, and the goat would look up at him, flick her ears forward, and turn her lips back. Once, he thought about taking her outside with him to enjoy the sun, but he remembered Mendel's warning and went out again to sit alone.

At lunch time, several men came to see the goat. They went into the shack, rubbed their chins, jingled coins in their pockets, muttered to themselves, counted on their fingers the cost of the ticket divided by the probability of their winning, and, usually, bought. Just before one, the parade ceased.

The sun turned to the west and began its decline. Shlomo dozed in a chair in front of the shack. A voice woke him. "Shlomo!"

Shlomo roused himself. "Standing at the gate was Sura, wife of the matchmaker.

"Hello," Shlomo said.

"Hello," said Sura.

"You're here to see..."

"No, I just thought I'd come to talk."

Shlomo was silent. Across the river, a tug shrieked.

"This lottery...this drawing...I was wondering...who was doing the drawing."

"Me, I guess."

"Ah."

"Mendel didn't say, but I thought..."

"Oh..."

Sura looked at the shack. "You lead a lonesome life here."

"I don't know...."

"You could use a wife, to cook, to clean, to mend your shirts."

"Who would marry me?"

"You never can tell."

Shlomo was suddenly uncomfortable. "You want to see the goat?"

Sura glanced at the sun. "No, I better be getting on." She paused. "You wouldn't happen to be going to services this evening?"

"I never thought."

"Well, goodbye." And she left.

Shlomo sat back in his chair.

The afternoon passed very slowly. The sun dropped behind the buildings. Shlomo began to think of services, of meeting human forms and hearing human voices. He closed the door of the shack and hurried to South Street where the men were already gathered. As he came into the room, the men parted to let him pass. He sat near the front, waiting silently for the service to begin.

He filled his memory with the sounds around him. At first, they were a low buzz, but suddenly there was a sharp sound just behind him. "Pssst, Shlomo."

He turned. "Pssst, Shlomo!" It was Ruben, the matchmaker. He leaned forward until his nose was almost in Shlomo's ear. "You've got a goat?" he hissed.

Shlomo nodded.

"And I've got a girl."

Shlomo frowned and turned around. "What?"

"Shhh. You want them to think there's monkey business going here?"

"What kind of girls?"

"Beautiful, of course. Smart, educated. Rich, no, but beautiful...."

"Why are you telling me?"

"Sura tells me you're lonesome."

"So?"

"And I want to help out...naturally...also Sura tells me you're doing the drawing of the ticket...I mean, if on the day of the drawing the Holy One, blessed be He, should look down and see that I have performed a good deed, perhaps His hand...."

"You want to buy a ticket, then?"

"Sure. Get me a lucky one." Ruben laughed and punched Shlomo's shoulder. "You know what I mean?"

When Shlomo returned, there were two small girls standing by the shack and staring at it. Their clothes were thin and sewn together in many places. "Who are you?" Shlomo said.

"Our Mama bought a ticket on the goat today. She sent us down to see you," one said.

"We're awful poor," the other joined in, "and the goat would help."

"We could get milk."

"And cheese."

Shlomo shook his head. "What do I have to do with this?"

"You're drawing the ticket, aren't you?"

"And it's your goat."

"But I take the ticket out of the bowl. That's what Mendel told me. I don't know whose ticket will come out. I don't even know your number."

"Seven."

"You could put it on top of the bowl..."

"After everybody's bought."

"But that's not what Mendel said."

"Oh."

The two turned from the gate and walked away.

Shlomo slept by the goat that night, with his hand on its back. Often, during the night, he frowned in his sleep; often his lips moved. Once or twice he stroked the goat's back. Toward morning, he began to toss, woke several times, and several times fell asleep. At six there was a rumbling outside his door. He rose slowly, shaking his head to clear the dizziness from it, walked to the door and threw it open.

Gathered infront of his shack was a large crowd. By the door there stood a boy in kneebreeches and cap with a paper-wrapped bundle in his arms. When he saw Shlomo come out of his shack, the boy rushed up and shoved the package into his hands. "It's a cake, homemade, my mother's. Number fifteen." He turned and ran away, into the crowd.

A woman pushed to the front. She carried a liver chicken by the legs. "Take it. My number is twenty-six!" She hurled the bird at Shlomo's feet.

At once, neighbor began to mutter to neighbor. The crowd started forward together. "Here's flour! Five pounds." one cried.

"I got some nice homemade candy here...number thirty!"

"Remember me, number six? I got a little money here."

Shlomo stood on the stoop, still holding the brown-wrapped cake in his arms. The gifts grew at his feet as people rushed up, deposited their offerings, shouted their number and disappeared.

Some pulled at his elbow. "I got three kids at home that could use the milk."

"I got four."

"I got five...ain't had milk for a week."

"Six!"

And then they were gone.

Shlomo stood alone. He looked out over his yard. The two thin girls stood, staring at Shlomo, the gifts, the open door through which they could make out the goat. They turned and were gone.

Shlomo folded onto the stoop, frightening the chicken and scattering the gifts. He put his head on his lap and began to cry. The goat came out of the house and brushed against him. Shlomo looked up. He patted her head, then pushed her away, off the stoop, toward the river. She paused for a moment to nibble at the sparse grass in front of the shack, then walked without pausing to the river. Shlomo made no motion to follow her. He watched dumbly as she paused at the edge of the river to look back at him. He nodded. She walked into the water. She sank at once and did not reappear.

And when Mendel finally came at ten, Shlomo said, "The goat is gone."

The Upscale Tour

THE FLOWERS ON THE STATE STREET BRIDGE, PINK AND RED AND white, flaunted themselves against the dull green of the window box and the bridgetender's house. Lyn made the flowers the first stop of her day-before-payday ritual, always pausing in the park to look at them while she considered how to spend this lunch hour-- where to wander, what to look at, how to blow the last of last week's check. Tossing those last few dollars into utter foolishness, that was the most important part. It left her feeling wealthy, jaunty, optimistic about whatever came next.

She had just about decided to take the upscale tour when she was accosted by the man in the Hawaiian shirt. His stick-thin arms, hanging beneath the garish brown and black and orange swirls that only a Goodwill store could love, warned her that the man was probably a resident of this area of grass and bricks and benches the guys at the office had named Wino Park. Still, this man's eyes seemed clear, his gait steady, and his words lucid. Too lucid. For he began to spin a sad tale of a sister in Janesville, so complete as to medical difficulties, sibling duty, imminent disaster and exact fare needed, that Lyn was digging in her skirt pocket before the man was halfway through. She was so mesmerized that she did not even wonder why the two dollar bills were in her pocket instead of in her purse.

She watched the man head off in the general direction of the Greyhound terminal, evaluating his route and posture. When he had disappeared, she turned her back on the park and strolled across the bridge toward Jefferson Street. The sky was a militantly clear September-blue, and the air was full of cruising butterflies and dragonflies riding the breezes like thumbsized heatwaves.

As always, when Lyn chose the upscale tour, she stopped first outside the window of the linen shop. Inspecting the draped and festooned merchandise, she found herself regretting that she was, at her core, a showerperson, who would never feel a need for monogrammed towels of sybaritic thickness. And it annoyed her to have to fight, as always, the coldhearted pragmatism that was chiding her for wasting precious time today.

So, in defiance, she strode into the showroom at the corner. She inspected the high, dark wood cases of leaded glass and place settings and silver upended like dancers in toeshoes, but they all cowed her, as they seemed to cow the other shoppers, into a churchlike stillness.

She turned her attention to the exhibit on the long mahogany table. She supposed they were staging some sort of homage to summer there. Lighthearted pink was the keynote: pink placemats and pink borders on the oriental china. The crystal had stems of glass-bamboo and the silverware handles were similarly decorated. In the center of the table, a miniature seashore replaced the requisite flowers. There was a sandcastle fashioned of bumpy tan ceramic, with a fair number of colorful seashells, artfully scattered. And all of this sat atop a genuine miniature beach. Her mother's voice was commenting inside Lyn's head--her mother, First Pragmatist of the family, who never let a single clot of dust lie noticed for longer than it took to fetch a rag. Her mother was saying what she thought about the strands of genuine sand, snaking in graceful patterns to the very tips of the silverware. Lyn knew at once that she had giggled aloud, and loudly. The face of the saleswoman who materialized at her shoulder informed her that, without question, she had rudely tampered with the unsolicited silence.

Her watch said that the Scheherazade of Wino Park had taken more of her hour than she'd realized. She told the saleswoman of her time problem--no need to mention the other here--and left, glad that a total lie had not been necessary.

But the leftover money nagged at her. She glanced around, wondering where she should go. Three young women were hurrying down the sidewalk toward Cathedral Square. They carried covered Styrofoam platters. The craving rose from these, seized her, and pulled her across the street, through the glass door, and down the red tiled steps. She could taste already how the tour would end. The taste of cheesecake was palpable.

There was a long line in front of the bakery counter. Lyn counted the people, wondering if she had the time to wait. There were thirty of them, but four clerks taking orders, taking money. She played a mathematical game, in part to keep from thinking of the next step, the only danger in the ritual. The rule was that she did not count her money till she'd spent it; it was this, more than anything else, that defined wealth for her. Yet this was not really dangerous as it seemed, for in the months she'd been doing it, she had developed a feeling, a gauge of her current solvency. Moreover, today she was certain that she was more flush than she'd ever been; this morning she had had reason to see an entire, unbroken, five dollar bill in her billfold. Not that she'd gone looking for it--that would be a violation of the game--but somewhere, someone had asked....The line was moving forward and she could feel, without looking back, that many people crowded in behind her. And now that she was close enough to see, the craving was building to an obsession. She hoped that the chalkboard might cure her foolishness by announcing that the cheesecake was unavailable today; instead, it added a dimension--chocolate. She had tasted that cake just once, at a birthday party. Someone there had called it a cake he'd kill for. At the time, Lyn had considered the remark a joke. But the party had been last December, and she could still taste that cake. There was, first, a glaze of chocolate, almost black in its richness, almost candy in its viscosity, but bittersweet, not cloying, and echoed by a thin layer of chocolate cake that held the whole thing up. In between was the cheesecake, whatever taste it possessed made almost imperceptable by the chocolate, so that the tongue was left with nothing but the essence of richness. And lurking beneath the glaze, yet permeating the whole, the liquid tartness of liqueur or raspberries--she had eaten it too fast to be able to choose.

She moved forward with the line, knowing that she must have something to drink. She examined the board. The cake would be $1.95. And ice tea? Fifty cents. No problem. Without a doubt the change she'd ignored all week would more than cover the tea and tax, and she would still have three dollar bills to squander.

She glanced behind her. The line was even longer than it had been when she joined it. People in an obvious hurry, men in business suits, women in new fall skirts and shirts.

The clerk asked; she answered as she'd planned--the cake, the tea. The clerk rang up the total, told her. She want into her billfold. Nothing there but old deposit slips. And a single yellow cleaner's tag.

But where was the five dollar bill? Lyn reconstructed, feeling, every second, the breath and hurry of the people behind her. To her right, another clerk was handing a narrow paper to a blonde in jeans. Beside the blonde, another who had money was taking his receipt. At work this morning someone--no time to think of who--had begged a contribution for the sick. And she had gone and--that was when she'd seen it--taken out the five and asked for two in charge. For now. For squandering. With change and this it would have been enough. She'd shoved them in her pocket. She'd taken them from there to finance a trip to Janesville.

What now to tell the clerk? Was there enough change at the bottom of her purse? There'd never been before.

Breath and hurry. Breath and hurry. She forced herself to smile, to say, "My conscience got the better of me. Forget the cake. I'll just be having tea. And artificial sweetner, if you have it."

She hoped she seemed fat enough to justify the lie.

The clerk tore up the bill without a comment. She rang up tea and handed Lyn the slip. The line waiting to redeem the narrow slips for food seemed very long, too long. Or so she told herself. She left the place, trying not to run.

And what could she make of the experience? What was she supposed to gain from it? Compassion, Lyn decided as she walked. She practiced compassioning as she walked. It beat humiliation.

She was almost back across the State Street bridge, had just taken note of the fact that it was harder to see the flowers from the bridge than from the park, when she spotted brown and black and orange swirls weaving between the halfgrown scotch pines that marched along the winding brick pathway in the park. It was, without question, the same man who had accosted her, and, without question, he was not in the condition he had been in when they'd parted. Had he made it to the hummock where he seemed to be heading, and had he settled down to sleep, Lyn would still have been aware of what had transpired, for his right hand clutched the transparent plastic binding that had once encircled a can of beer. In fact, had once encircled a full six pack, two-sixths of which remained, dangling from his hand.

Without thinking, without seeming to run, Lyn came off the bridge and stood between him and the hummock. She pulled herself up to her full height and loomed above him, glaring down at him. In her mother's voice, she said, "You son of a bitch! You told me you had a sick sister in Janesville. Look at you. You should be ashamed of yourself, telling lies and then getting drunk."

Without seeming to register any emotion, or even any understanding of what she had told him, the man reached out and hung the plastic circle on Lyn's still-outstretched admonishing forefinger. Then, as she stood there wondering if he meant her to have what remained of the beer, she realized that he was digging into the pocket of his ragged pants. Wordlessly, he handed over two crumpled dollar bills, repossessed his beer, gave one last sad glance at the hummock in the pines and, walking around her with the cans cradled against his chest, he shambled off across the bridge toward Jefferson Street.

She knew that she must hurry if she meant to be on time. Still, she watched him go, knowing she had left a large and important component out of what she'd said to him. She had left out herself. She had lied to him, as surely as she had lied to herself about her ritual.

And once again she damned the man. For that hurt less than thinking of whatever came next.

Christmas Brown

HEY FOLDED <u>The Herald</u> ON ME JUST WHEN I'D LEARNED THEIR damned machine. So there I was, three months out of J-school, full of the writing courses and the requisite regard for Truth, well-supplied with cynicism and a vocabulary my mother never knew, and out of a job.

Me and 25 other journalism graduates, who didn't know a sinking ship when it hired them.

The others scurried homeward. But I stuck around, looking for something that might draw on one or more of the talents I'd acquired.

It was the damned machine that got me hired at the Superior Catholic Printing Company.

The interview was relatively painless. They asked me the usual, and then they asked my religion. I returned casually, "Why should that matter?" as if it was not a question I'd been expecting as soon as I saw the name.

They expressed surprise, undoubtedly a lot more genuine than mine, so I went on, as rehearsed, plugging in the hesitations where I felt they ought to be, batting my eyes and lifting the hem of my get-a-job skirt. I told them they'd advertised for a proofreader, and I'd been taught that meant they wanted somebody who would only change the dictionary and grammar book mistakes, not alter content. And then I laid on the most ingenuous smile in my collection.

And then one of the men asked if I could run a VDT. Asked as if I was going to request a definition, as if he already knew the answer was no. So I pointed to my three months on <u>The Herald</u>--not hard to find in a short résumé. They called me the next day, Thursday, to say that I was hired.

Since they hadn't persisted with their question about my religion, I hadn't argued over working conditions. A fair trade. Which is how I found myself reporting for work at five o'clock the next Monday afternoon.

Days, SCPC handled the heavy stuff, the Catholic books and other things that lasted. Evenings was when the transitory got done, mostly church bulletins that came to their suburban warren from parishes throughout the Midwest.

The men I'd met on Wednesday shepherded me to the room where their two VDT's had just been installed and left me in the hands of a woman who knew less than I did. Her name was Eileen. I never knew her last name. I'm bad at listening when people give me names; I never expect what's coming.

Before the arrival of the machines, the small room had been used to store things. Was still. Giant rolls of paper, yellowish newsprint for the poorer parishes, better quality, somewhat whiter stock for the richer. Pre-printed four-color covers for all of them, then reams of paper in stacks.

Cans of ink, upended, made pyramids in two corners. Mysterious, unmarked cartons in even rows almost obscured a useless door. In fact, all four walls of the small room were virtually hidden by things. Even the windows were hidden by things. Which, considering the hours we worked, meant nothing.

The air in the small room came blowing through the single open doorway from the main floor of the plant, where the presses were, then was pushed around our room by a fan on a tall stand. Occasionally a breeze would lift a stray paper from one of the piles.

And that was a primary diversion. The truth is, by the end of the second week, I had gotten tired of resting my eyes by cataloging the contents of the walls which, probably because things got brought in and brought out only during the day, never seemed to change. And so, by default, I spent a lot of my time, when my eyes weren't on the machine, paying attention to Eileen.

Before the machines, the light in the small room had consisted of a single bare bulb. Now, added to this was the chartreuse glow of the twin television screens, which spread past the keyboards beneath them, then not much further than our chairs. The day they brought me to the room, they were promising more lights. They were still promising more lights the day I left.

This Eileen was as pale as the cave we worked in. That pallor sprang from working as many night hours here as she could grab, then spending day hours in the house with chores and children. And whatever other hours, caught at random, for sleep. I saw the pallor at once; in the low light of that small room, there was a sort of phosphorescent glow about Eileen. But it took a while to understand it.

She was relieved to see someone who could teach her the machines. There had been eight other women--girls, she called them--and they'd all worked in a large room at the front, reading weekly messages, announcements of births and deaths, and lists of names and contributions to one another from the papers sent from churches and the papers printed elsewhere in the plant. Last Thursday, they'd been told how these new machines would make everything easier, get rid of the paper and the endless reading aloud. On Friday, the others had been given their notice.

Eileen did not seem to regard herself as some kind of winner, or take her survival as a compliment. Her only emotion seemed to be anxiety about keeping the job. She needed the night work, she told me. Then she had her daytime hours for her children. That is what she said.

There were seven children, five boys, two girls. The oldest would be 14 in mid-March. The youngest was almost three. I never knew the names of more than four. And you have to understand that it was not Eileen who added all these figures up for me. And you have to understand that she never talked of those children in a lump, but only one at a time, stretched out over the six months I knew her.

The part of the job Eileen did know, she was master at. The painstaking checking for minute errors, for one letter missing, one comma out of place. She could quote rules I'd never heard of, not in four years of college, rounded off by a grammar competency test. Eileen just smiled and blamed the nuns.

You have to understand that we did not talk much in that room, not about my college career or anything else. Probably it was because the throw and clatter of the presses never stopped coming through the open door till ten o'clock at night, and by then Eileen would be so into working that no one could break her concentration.

Some time in the six months, she did mention that she had married just out of high school, and that the 14-year-old had been born before her first wedding anniversary. So she must have been no more than ten years older than I was.

Yes, Eileen knew more rules, but I showed her the machinery. She had been told that the words got into a computer memory when other hands typed them, and that a lot of the Chicago parishes, having access to terminals there, sent their stuff over telephone wires.

At the point I arrived, she could stare at the cold green words and see where changes should be made. But her hands did not know how to break into what she saw on the screen.

Sometime that first night, I taught her how to accomplish whatever they wanted at SCPC. Of course, far less was required of her than they'd asked for at The Herald. We did not gather facts, or put our facts in order or revise. All we could do, really, was check words over, change whatever mistakes we could find, then punch a button and command it all to the inevitability of print. If that was not as careful as it had been in the world of paper to paper, SCPC did not seem to mind.

Sometime that first night, needing a break, Eileen asked me how I had gotten there. I replied, "I lost my other job."

She smiled sadly and said, "You're lucky. I think they're making me lose my faith." Then sat back down and started concentrating on the screen, started practicing again the motions I had showed her, afraid, I guess, that her fingers might forget.

I first encountered Chrismas Brown about three weeks after I started at SCPC. It was shortly after the presses fell silent, and I was taking an unauthorized break, pacing the small space, rubbing the pain in my neck, trying to rid myself of the pink spots that inevitably appeared before my eyes when I'd been staring at the screen too long. I was feeling punchy and looking for amusement.

Eileen was still at her screen. She sighed. In the sudden silence it was a loud sigh, and such emotion, for her, was completely out of character. Torn away from perusing the walls, I moved quickly behind her.

She was staring at a list of names that stretched from the top of the screen to the bottom. To the right of each name was an amount of money. Since I, too, had gone over such lists, I knew that above these names, and below them, in the ether of the computer's memory, there would be many more, endless names, and moneys. These were the contributions that had come to the parish the previous Sunday. Once, when Eileen had been in an owly mood, she'd expressed mild dissatisfaction, saying that when she was a child, every church published such a listing, but now only a few were doing it.

The names on the screen that night, Eileen explained to me, were members of a poor black parish in Chicago. It was one of the worst, Eileen said, but instead of explaining that, she rose and let me stare at the screen while she paced around, trying to rid herself of her own cramps and spots.

About midway down the lefthand side of the screen I encountered Chrismas Brown. My right hand jumped to punch the insert key. My left forefinger rested on the keyboard's "t." But when Eileen saw what I was planning, she stopped me. "It's right," she said. "I called down there and checked on it two years ago."

"But what made you guess?"

She ran her finger down the screen. "Alphabetical order," she said.

I looked again at the misspelled name, and then began to laugh. You have to understand that there wasn't a whole lot to laugh about in that place. "You mean her mother didn't know how to spell it? That word?"

I wasn't exactly surprised that Eileen did not laugh, but the grimness on her face was a lot colder than anything I had ever seen there before. "Didn't they box it when it was coming in on paper?" I asked.

"Box it? What does that mean?"

I found a stray piece of paper on the floor. I printed the name as it appeared on the screen, which was damned hard to do. And then I drew a careful rectangle around the misspelled word.

"What does that mean?" The same words, and the same gripped compulsion in the voice, as if we were talking about two different things.

I tried to drag her into my mood. I smiled and shrugged and said, "You box a word to make it stand out for the printer. In this case, it means, 'Don't fuck aroun' with Chrismas Brown'"

I knew the obscenity would get her. I knew what a lady she was. You could tell by looking at her neatly combed hair and her ironed dresses and her stockings--even on the hottest September nights in that sticky little room, and the two of us the only ones around!

Still, she did not berate me for my language; instead she pointed across the screen to the place where the woman's contribution was listed in the middle of the rest. To the place where the amount was. The others had given a dollar or two dollars or three.

And Chrismas Brown had given 50 cents.

"No need for anybody to box that," she said coldly. "It stands out without any help."

I laughed again, because those two digits looked so naked standing there. But Eileen was hanging on to her grimness. "I think about her sometimes. Who she might be. I imagine she's an old lady, and she has to save and save just to get that much together. Because she doesn't give it every week, you see. She only has it every two or three."

"Maybe she only makes it to church every other week," I said, slipping into Eileen's fantasy for lack of anything better to do. "Maybe those other weeks she's too busy."

"Doing what?"

"Who knows. Going to the movies. Scrubbing floors. Getting laid." I was really getting into it now. "Sure, that's got to be it. The 50 cents is her idea of a commission."

Eileen was definitely not laughing. "Maybe she avoids church so she doesn't have to see herself in the bulletin."

"If she didn't want to read about it, she wouldn't give at all," I snapped, bored with the thing. "Don't you have anything else to worry about?"

Eileen sat down abruptly and began to scroll up so that new names would appear on the screen. Her seriousness was a downer, and the pink dots were not fading for me. I didn't want to return to work, so I reached over to her keys. "Wait a minute," I told her. "Since this really bothers you, I'll show you how to do something about it."

I brought old Chrismas back onto the screen. I put the machine into the insert mode. A line of red dots lit up along the right side of the keyboard, a warning. I moved the cursor until it filled the space and let it sit there for a second. The little rectangle winked impatiently at me, saying, "Okay, already, let's get at it." Twice I hit the "erase character" key. The space and the decimal point blinked away. I hit the right arrow and moved the cursor off the five. I inserted a new decimal point and a second zero.

You have to understand that this all took a lot less time to do than to tell about. It was fast. It was easy. And the best part was that without a paper record, there was nothing left to show that it had ever been another way. Now old Chrismas's contribution took up as much space as the others' and outdid theirs in size.

I returned to my machine and let Eileen wrestle with the idea of playing God, or whatever the hell she thought it was.

The months passed and Halloween and Thanksgiving came. I used my mornings for sleeping and my afternoons for exploring the city and my evenings for earning my keep. More for amusement than anything else, I began to bait Eileen when we'd take our breaks, began to play off this prim lady-ness of hers.

I remember once, for instance, doing a few manic minutes on the magic of "motherfucker," as it had once been explained by a friend in college, a physics major, I recall. What you did was, you took whatever inanimate object was giving you grief, and you called it that. And by magic, it suddenly became light enough to lift or responsive enough to work for you, or whatever. It seems to me that I even demonstrated on one of the cans of ink.

You have to understand that this was not one of the more intensely interesting periods of my life. In fact, I even would sometimes ask after old Chrismas, but Eileen only worked away silently.

The churches were holding their own, I guess, for SCPC had the same work as always, no more, no less. I'd arrive every night in my jeans, and there she would be in her skirt and stockings. The skirts turned to wool in cold weather, but I don't know that they were any more protection for her legs when it started dropping near zero.

91

The first weekend in January ended in a massive snowstorm that closed the whole area down for two days. On the third evening, when SCPC opened at last, I came in late. But Eileen was later still. The pallor was more phosphorescent than usual, and there was an even more drawn, more harried look about the lips.

She would not explain herself, though that was not extraordinary. But after a while I heard that sigh, that same sigh that had introduced me to Chrismas Brown.

I looked over her shoulder. The lady was on the screen again, except that the typist in Chicago had gone and inserted the "t." Eileen said, out of nowhere, "That box was good protection. Like an umbrella. Wouldn't it be nice if we could all walk around in a box?"

Because I could not believe that misspelling a misspelled name could cause anybody such grief, I looked elsewhere, to the right of the screen. Chrismas had contributed $1.50 this week. "Changed it again," I joked.

"I don't change anything." It was all she said to me for the rest of the night.

So January passed, and February. Then late that month, late one Friday night, close to midnight, when I was spaced out with fatigue and overcome by the desire for the weekend to begin, I heard that sigh one last time.

I went over to Eileen's screen, expecting to find Chrismas come again. But she was not there. Charles Brown was listed, and then Christian Brown. Alphabetical. The thing she'd seen that meant the "t" was rightly gone. A small thing; Eileen was so good at making sense of small things.

"She hasn't been in church in three weeks."

"The weather's been rotten," I responded. "It's been even worse in Chicago."

"No, that's not it. I forced her into giving more than she could afford."

"You don't know that!"

She did not seem to have heard me. "She'd been coming every week since I let that change go through. And she'd been giving every week. Sometimes a dollar, sometimes more. She probably decided that God was trying to tell her something. So every week she came and gave."

I began to fear the passion in her voice. "Maybe she's doing better... at whatever she was doing." I made a conscious effort not to leer.

Stubbornly, Eileen shook her head.

I scratched my memory, shook something free. "The widow's mite--doesn't it say somewhere--don't you believe--that a person gets more credit...."

"Not in that parish! In that parish the priest demands that you give first to God and then worry about the gas company bill. Because it's God who takes care of us." Bitterly she laughed, then repeated, "It's God who takes care of everything." And then she added, "I believe that Mrs. Brown froze to death."

"You are making that up. Your imagination is running off with your reason."

"The hell I'm making it up! I proofread his damned column. He runs it every December."

The profanity should have warned me that she was out over the edge and going down, but I know Eileen far better now.

But what I did know--too well--that night was that a sleet storm had begun just as I was coming to work; I had been worrying about driving home, and Eileen's hysteria was not doing anything for my nerves. So I told her that she should go home early, for by now there was no one around but us. I told her I'd punch her card before I left. She got up and went.

Saturday. Sunday. I came in Monday night, but Eileen was not there. Nor was she there on Tuesday. One of the men stayed late on Wednesday, late enough to talk to me. He promised to hire somebody else. He seemed to assume that I knew where Eileen was.

On Friday, a handsome fortyish man was in the small room when I arrived. He was sitting in my chair. When he stood to greet me, he seemed to fill the place, for he was so healthy looking in that gloom, so vigorous, so lusty, irresistible. I wondered for a brief moment if such a man could be Eileen's replacement.

And then he introduced himself as her husband. And said he'd come to repossess her things.

"But why isn't she coming back?" I demanded.

Tears came to his eyes. "You must be the new girl they've hired to replace her. I really wanted the other," he said after a bit.

"I am the other." I waited.

"She went off a bridge near here last Friday. Off a bridge so fast she broke through the ice. They didn't find the car till Saturday morning."

"An accident," I insisted, worrying briefly that had I not released her, Fate would not have pushed her in.

He shook his head. "It wasn't slippery. Not that late. The sanders had been out all night. It wasn't slippery."

I felt his pain. "You believe suicide's a sin," I protested.

He searched my face, wondering how much to share with me. He said, "They did an autopsy. She was almost two months pregnant. My father kept asking me, all those years, 'How can you let her work so much?'" He stopped, shook his head, asked, "That's a different generation, isn't it?"

He asked then for her things. There was not much: a dictionary with her name in front that I hadn't seen her use in the six months I knew her; a spare sweater; several papers in the table drawer beneath her machine. He sifted through those papers, pulled one out, asked if I knew the meaning. It was my printing, Chrismas's name, the box. Protection, I had said. And she had said, how nice to be so safe. Had said it...I thought back...just after that January storm that kept her home and him home all at once.

I looked at the box. It looked now like a coffin. I explained the printers' meaning of the box. He left.

They hired a new girl out of high school, a girl who wore a miniscule engagement ring and bubbled about her impending marriage. I did not last another month. I found a reporting job in another state, a daytime job besides.

I like collecting other people's facts. I like arranging them and putting them into the machine.

Proofreading was the world's biggest bore. Creating would be a pain in the ass.

Someone To Hear

"THERE'S THIS ABOUT REPORTERS," BOB MARTIN SAID. "ASK what they're doing and they'll talk for hours. About every unprinted detail they've learned just so they can understand what's going on, every detail the readers didn't need to know or wouldn't want to. And reporters will talk about how they feel, because that doesn't ever get in print, not if they're any good."

At the end of Betsy Heid's first night on the New Ralston Register, Martin invited her to join him at the Thirty Bar, next door to the paper, but when she arrived, the city editor was already holding forth beneath the Old Style clock with its electric cascade and dial that showed one forty five. The Thirty was the only place still open.

Uncomfortable with the attention she was attracting as the newcomer, Betsy kept glancing at the group of reporters and editors gathered around Martin, wondering why he had bothered to invite her here if he meant to ignore her. The three obituaries she'd written that night hardly merited the lecture he was delivering.

She watched the face beneath the thick, greying hair, animated when he spoke, neutral as he listened. "Kind lines" her mother had called spider webs like the ones at the edges of his eyes and lips. Betsy chastised herself for misunderstanding his invitation.

She would write obituaries and weather stories for five weeks before she hit a day like Martin had described, never, until the Fourth of July, accumulating the burdensome leftover facts he'd talked about. But on that day, with most of the regulars off, she was assigned to cover

95

the holiday, then compress it into nine and a half inches of copy. Was required to describe the parade, and the kids, and the bands, and the dog dressed like the Statue of Liberty who won Best Dressed at the Lions' barbeque, and the fireworks, the last burst of which fell onto the mayor's roof instead of into the river. The roof was still in flames when Betsy squeezed what she could into her story and escaped to the Thirty where Martin had the grace to hear her out without reminding her that he knew what she was doing.

"There's too much slopping over," Betsy complained. "And all of it good stuff. The suitcase was too small."

"I have to assert myself somehow," Martin shrugged. He added that any good story would seem that way; she shouldn't be bothered.

"Weren't you bothered when you were a reporter?"

"That wasn't so many years ago," he protested. "You might as well know, though, that you gave me fourteen inches. I cut the dog." He pointed out the window. "Go home and get some sleep," he said. "That glow you see is not the mayor's house. It's sunrise."

When someone else was hired, Betsy was transferred to features: neighborhood beat-the-heat-athons; doll buggy parades; the first day of school at a local nursery; the arrival of the second bear at New Ralston's one-bear zoo. When they saw that she could do well at features, they promoted her to substituting for the beat reporters. Betsy endured the meetings, wringing readable stories from her notes, then trading her unused and, occasionally unpublishable, anecdotes at the Thirty with the others from the Register.

War stories, Bob Martin called them. He always seemed to sit in on Betsy's group, saying little. At first he'd hang on after she left, but early in October he began to leave whenever she did and walk her back to the furnished room she'd rented till something better came along.

The room was so small that the door to the street almost hit her armchair and the door to the bathroom did bump against her bed if she moved it far enough from the chair to leave room for a sitter's knees. After the first time Martin walked her home, Betsy made sure that her books and papers were neatly stacked on her dresser top and all her clothes were shoved into drawers or closets before she left for work.

After the third time, she stopped bothering; Martin never asked to come inside and Betsy was too confused to know if she cared.

He would never tell her if he'd liked the things she'd written that night; she told herself on bad nights that this saved her ego. But sometimes, in the next morning's paper, there would be a byline, a "by Betsy Heid." She knew that awarding bylines was often like tipping for good service, and that, for all the socializing he did with her--with them--at the Thirty, he was the boss who made that decision.

Betsy was scheduled to work both Christmas and New Year's, eves and days. She only knew newspaper people here, and they weren't complaining about working. Besides, her salary would not cover the two thousand mile journey she'd have to make to find someone who'd want to see her.

But Grace the switchboard operator overheard her remarking to someone that she welcomed the assignment because important news might break on a holiday. It was time, Grace said, to take Betsy in hand and find her some normal male who would make her care about the things that counted in the outside world.

Introducing Betsy out there was not a simple matter. The New Ralston Register came out seven mornings a week. The civilized days off were given by seniority; Betsy had every Monday and Thursday to herself.

With much fanfare, Grace set her up with a high school teacher, a cousin's cousin's friend. Grace touted him as cute and bright and single. He was also late when he picked Betsy up the Monday after New Year's, and disgruntled. Without giving her a chance to ask, he replayed the faculty meeting that had gone on much too long.

Betsy could still remember how things were handled in the outside world. Forcing interest, she asked what important thing had kept them late. Running through her memories of the two school board meetings she had covered, she inquired if it had been some burning question of, say, curriculum or discipline. His mouth full of spaghetti, he informed her that there were no burning questions. Ever. Except for salary. And ending meetings when they were supposed to end.

She let him get her home at ten o'clock, which would have been her supper break at work. He was yawning.

At one, the time Bob Martin usually came into the Thirty, Betsy took a walk downtown.

There was an afternoon when the city editor was two hours late. Betsy asked about it after work. "At least they're teaching you to be observant," he snapped. "At these prices, that's a good thing."

"Beer's cheap here," she retorted.

"Maybe you haven't learned much at that. I'm talking about your job. About my job. About this crummy midnight ghetto we've all moved into."

"I don't mind."

"Who've you met so far? One yawning clown? Listen up. Some day you'll find somebody and try to settle down. You'll find out how the rest of the world gets on. And when."

"You never said you felt that way," Betsy protested.

"Of course not. You were too busy talking. But that's okay. It's an occupational hazard."

"Like being a stand-in uncle? Well, okay, Uncle, what would you have told me if I'd shut up?"

Bob Martin winced, drained his beer glass, inspected the bottom, said, "Just, get out while you can. Before you're hooked. Before some stranger lets you know you've touched him with some story you've worked hard on. Find a teacher. Hell, find any kind of civilian. There are other businesses where people care what they're doing. Just, get away from this one. See, once upon a time, I had a wife and kids."

"I heard. Until last year."

He shrugged, continued, "Well, I was living nights. They weren't. I thought we were making it up on Tuesdays and Fridays. But then my son started school so, mornings, I'd be sleeping when he left. If we got lucky, I'd see him to wave to as he was walking home and I was driving off. He took to waking himself up at two a.m. when he'd hear me come in, just so we could talk a little bit. My wife kept waiting for it to make a difference. It did. But not as much as handling stories that might change the world. Or wake up New Ralston. Or wrap somebody's fish." He laughed. "New Ralston. Ever contemplate the name?"

Betsy shook her head.

"Well, kid, where you are working is a town named in memory of some other town. Except nobody ever heard of the other town but the guy who moved out here. Big deal!"

"Where'd you go for the job interview this morning?"

He stared at her.

"Blame it on my training. You ask about what they don't say," Betsy explained, "and if they don't hit you, you get a story."

"It's a mobile occupation," Martin said. "People move on. Sometimes on their own, sometimes because somebody else gives them a leg up. Sometimes because they get lucky and defect to something else."

It took Grace a month to find Betsy a second date, a stockbroker, a friend of a friend. It was not herself, Grace assured Betsy, but her hours that the men found unpalatable. The stockbroker sounded promising on the phone. Betsy agreed to meet him for lunch on Thursday.

The police reporter called in sick on Wednesday afternoon. Betsy had been hanging around the office, waiting for an assignment. She was still hanging around at nine that night, waiting for her first emergency, when the fire department scanner went off.

The farm was a half-mile from the main highway, up a winding, rutted township road. The buildings that the fire had not destroyed were ancient and tilting on their foundations. They needed care as well as paint, Betsy thought, but she wrote, "Barn, two sheds, corn crib one third full." The fire had been burning since eight thirty, the local chief told her. Four rural fire departments were there. He gave her the names, provided the spellings when she asked. She could see no story in this unimportant, rundown place, was about to radio back and leave, when she noticed a lanky man in overalls standing close to the heat of the blaze, staring into it. She asked the chief his name and occupation. "Well, that's their father," he responded.

"Whose?"

"The five kids that got trapped inside."

It was, by then, ten o'clock. The chief had walked away. Betsy thought to herself: there is this about people with unbearable tales: ask them and they'll talk for hours. She felt coldhearted; she felt mercenary; she felt the pressure of her deadline.

She drew close to the farmer and the fire that had been his home. She opened her jacket, flipped her notebook to a new page. "What happened?" she asked him.

The story flowed out of him. Their mother had gone off the week before. He'd been down in the barn tonight, milking. The kids had been asleep upstairs, or maybe they had. Maybe something'd happened with the woodstove. Or their chimney--he hadn't had the time to clean it out. Or maybe one of the kids liked matches and their ma had known and hadn't said. It was told without passion, as if all his passion had died with his wife's leaving, or with his children's deaths. But when he finished his account, he began to cry, then walked away.

It was not a story Betsy could phone in. Speeding to the office, she composed the words in her head. At the typewriter she found that the story came as if it were being dictated. The rundown farm, the farmer in his overalls, the children, his wording as he told her.

"I don't know what I would have done if he hadn't walked away," Betsy said to Bob Martin in the Thirty. "Because if he'd stayed, it would've looked bad when I didn't stick around to comfort him. But deadline's eleven thirty, after all."

The city editor smiled at her for the first time she could remember. Smiled and took her home. "It was a hell of a story," he told her at her door. "Grace says you've got a big lunch date. Remember what I said. Grab it if you can."

The stockbroker's knocking woke her. When she opened the door, he was standing with her morning paper in his hand. Waving him to her chair, she disappeared into the bathroom to dress. When she came out again, he was reading. She had to clear her throat to get his attention. "Quite an article," he said, holding the paper up so that she could see the banner headline stretching across the top of the front page. "Elizabeth A. Heid," he read. "That's you, isn't it?"

Unfortunately, it was the last thing he said to her that mattered, she told Bob Martin at the Thirty. He'd talked a lot about how she should invest her salary. When she'd broken in to protest that there wasn't much salary to talk about, he'd switched to the history of how he'd invested his own.

Still, he was a handsome man. And young, Betsy said, examining Martin's face for a reaction she did not find. But she did owe Grace something. So she'd agreed to go out with him again.

She had put on her best ironic smile to tell Martin about the stockbroker, but when she was through he asked, "What are you upset about?"

The smile slipped off. She propped her left elbow on the table and rested her forehead in the palm of her left hand. "It's the fire. Bob, they were pulling out the kids when I left."

"There's that, kid, and besides, you're worried because you think you used the farmer to get a story. Well, you didn't. You didn't steal anything from him. You didn't even have to prod him. You told me that yourself last night, how all you had to do was ask. How you must have been the first to ask and stick around to hear."

"But it meant so little, Bob. The stockbroker...he was impressed, for all of three minutes."

"It was a good story. There'll be more." In his voice there was a note of commiseration, of regard, and of nostalgia.

"You remember your first deaths," she said.

"Who wouldn't, kid?" Like a grownup comforting a child, Martin began to pat her shoulder.

Betsy shook off his hand. "I'm not a kid," she flared. "You've been avoiding that, but we both know you know it."

"What makes you so sure?"

"The byline," she shrugged. "You grew me up in print." She began to chuckle, then to smile. "I feel arrived."

"Let me walk you home," he said. "Tomorrow's my last day."

"I know. They told me."

Without Bob Martin, the conversations at the Thirty seemed tepid. Betsy found herself pitching in her stories, but caring as little about who she told them to as she would have cared about whether her garbage can was listening to her trash. She found herself longing for more space, for a room where she could have her own furniture, for a kitchen, for a table. She thought about renting an apartment in New Ralston. She thought about the pointless midnight ghetto at the Thirty.

She typed a letter. Trying to keep it light, she greeted him as Uncle. She typed, "Write when you've found me work."

She addressed the envelope to Martin, in care of the afternoon newspaper where he worked. She put her letter in the envelope, then took it out again. She read it over once more and crossed out the "Uncle." She retyped it.

She mailed it and sat back to wait.

The World's Greatest Carnival

A BIRD CHUCKLED IN THE BUSH NEAR THE KITCHEN WINDOW. Next door, half a block away, a power mower gnawed at the afternoon silence. Mike stopped printing and listened. A mile behind the high whining was the muted roar of the freeway, but that was all. There were no kid sounds. Mike frowned.

"Come on! Come on! We don't have all day." David reached across the table toward the thick black crayon. "If you don't want to do it, let me!" He lunged and grabbed.

"No, that's okay." Mike began to print again, his tongue stuck out of the corner of his mouth, but suddenly, without explanation, he balled up the sheet of paper and threw it into a corner.

"What's the matter? Did you forget the words?" David lurched toward him again. "It's World's Greatest Carnival--Come One Come All and Bring Your Money."

Mike smoothed out a new sheet. "If we paste on the picture you brought, that'll be too much," he said.

"If you could've walked over like last year, I might of picked out a different one." David subsided and began to stare at the vast stretch of Mike's new lawn.

Ignoring his eyes, Mike observed, "Everybody always says comeonecomeall."

"Then what should we put?" David took a long pull on his soda, the way he'd seen his father do it.

Mike lifted the paper Disneyland castle, pastel in the moonlight, and positioned it on the paper. Then he made a box with his hands. "After we put on World's Greatest Carnival, we only have this much left, see? Just enough for my address and the time, ten till two."

David looked worried. "Your mom said ten till noon," he corrected.

"She already said she's gonna be at her meeting. Besides, last year they stayed at your house till three."

"Last year was a blast, wasn't it?" David took a handful of popcorn and tossed one kernel at a time into his mouth. "I never saw half those kids before in my life!"

"Me either." Mike pushed himself away from the poster and smiled at the memory. "They covered your whole yard."

David frowned at his friend and at his big lawn.

"Hey, last year was great!" Mike cried, putting out a hand. "And all the moms that came, and the laughing. And remember how we didn't even get around to talk to them all?"

"I remember how they loved the games." David's eyes had shifted, glazing, focusing past the grass now, far beyond the borders of this big new house to last July. "And how they all waited in line for hours, just to play!"

"That was a good idea you had, adding the beanbag toss."

"Wish you could have helped make it, instead of Jerry."

Mike twirled the crayon between his fingers. "Who's Jerry?" he asked, his eyes on the shiny blackness.

"The kid who moved in next door to me. I told you on the phone. He's a friend of Paul's, the guy in your house, and they're both friends of...."

"If we're gonna get this poster put up so we get some kids, we better get going." A frown settled on Mike's face. Wordlessly, he picked up the glue, turned the picture over, and began to rub the cap around its edges.

"Are you sure we should hang it in your supermarket?" David had slipped behind the other's chair to look at the poster right side up.

Mike flipped the picture and smoothed it carefully on the paper. "The moms'll see it. They're always looking for something for their kids to do out here." Quickly now he printed out David's words.

David sprang for the door before the last word was finished. "Okay! Let's get going!" he shouted.

Mike rolled the poster and followed him, listening again. The mower had stopped; the traffic had slowed. Wasn't there anything in this crummy neighborhood but birds?

David walked down the aisle once before deciding he was not happy with the new store. "It's not gonna be like last year," he complained. "Our Winkie's has more things. And they're a lot cheaper."

"We saved five dollars from last year for prizes," Mike told him.

"Yeah, but I didn't think we'd have to spend it all."

"I never came in here before," Mike defended himself. "Besides, my mom was too busy to drive me to your house. I told you that."

"Why'd you have to move anyway?"

Mike shrugged. He stopped and fingered several toys on the counter. "Besides...." he began, then paused and thought about how to say this. "Maybe the kids out here expect the kind of prizes...from here."

"Oh?" There was a little anger in David's voice.

"Well, sure." Mike smiled to reassure him and picked up a rubber ball in a clear plastic box. "Now this is practically like the one we found at Winkie's last year, remember?"

David nodded.

"Remember how Tom won that one in the candle shoot, after he squirted Kathy in the face?"

Despite himself, David giggled. "And did she ever deserve it!" he added.

"And here's a paddleball. We can get this too. It's almost like the one we gave that new kid."

"Which one?"

"The guy who won for getting the best score of everybody."

"No, I mean, what did he look like?"

Mike noticed that David had picked up the paddleball and was taking some time to inspect it. "The funny-looking kid with the white hair and braces," he answered.

"Oh, you mean Jerry's friend Eddie. We play football a lot with him in the park." David had put down the paddleball and picked up a

105

puzzle. He turned it over to look at the price tag. "It's a dollar twenty nine," he told Mike. "That's a lot. But maybe we can use it for a big prize. Maybe highest score by two o'clock or something."

"Yeah, maybe." Chastened, Mike nodded, took the puzzle and tucked it under his arm. "We better get home," he said, strolling down the aisle, picking up toys without looking at them.

"What's the rush?" David called, hurrying after. "Hey, take your time. This part is almost as much fun as the carnival. Hey, look at this doll." He thrust the doll toward Mike's back, deliberately bumping him. "We oughta have some girl prizes, don't you think?"

Mike made a disgusted face. "I guess we might get some girls," he conceded.

"Remember that little blond kid from your block? The one that won all the games three times?"

"Nah, I don't remember," Mike said, putting on a swagger to cover up the memory of her head of spun-gold. He turned to take a closer look at the doll. It was small and crudely made, its hair more wig than hair and oozing dried glue, its dress a scrap of brown rag tied onto its body with a fraying red string. He took the doll from David's outstretched hand and added it to the collection. "It'll be okay for girls," he said.

When they returned to Mike's new house, they wrapped each prize in tissue paper. Then they discussed the games again. "Why don't you want the penny toss?" David asked.

"Well, it's okay, I guess. But we have to make it harder. Like...." He squinted his eyes and tried to recall a game he'd seen at State Fair. "If we can find our old laundry tub and float some bowls in the water and put numbers on them...."

"We could add the score and when they got to a thousand...."

"Better make it less," Mike cautioned.

"Why?"

"Because otherwise it'll take too long and the rest of the kids will get bored waiting in line."

"They didn't last year." David paused and looked out the window. Then he continued, "I guess you're right. I guess maybe the kids out here are different."

"Yeah." Pushing aside his growing uneasiness, Mike made work of racing around the kitchen, looking in cupboards he hadn't learned for the soup bowls he wasn't sure they'd brought along.

David woke Mike at five o'clock. By eight, the games had been set up. The coin toss was close to the water tap, the candles in their bottles were lined up on the picnic table, and a carton with multi-colored circles sat on top of the birdbath all the way across the lawn. "Geez, you're lucky to have all this room," David told Mike. "I guess I'm glad you talked me into having the carnival here."

Nodding his agreement, Mike began to pace off the distance from the wash tub. Ten feet away, he began to lay a string across the grass. "That's not far enough," David objected. "If a guy like that Eddie comes along, he'll get a hundred points in a minute, and we'll run out of prizes right away."

"It's far enough," Mike insisted.

"No it's not. Those prizes took all our money."

Mike looked from the tub to the string. "Tell you what--let's try it."

The suggestion seemed reasonable, so David took a penny from his pocket, stepped behind the string and pitched at the tub. The penny fell short. David tried another. He wound up and wound up and threw hard, but the coin fell short again.

Now Mike stepped up to the line. He pitched a hard one, which clanked against the rim of the 25 dish. "Told you it was right," he said smugly. "Now I'll try again." He wound up and tossed, and this time the penny landed in 10.

"No fair!" David shouted. "It's my turn." He picked up his pennies from the grass and returned to the string, spreading his feet wide, grinding his heels into the lawn. Then he threw overhand. The penny clinked against the outside of the 10 dish. "Hey, this is really fun! I forgot how much fun it was! How many points do you have so far?"

But Mike had other things on his mind. "We forgot about passing out announcements," he said.

"What announcements?"

"Remember last year when we rode around the neighborhood and gave out papers about the carnival?"

"Yeah, but we didn't have a supermarket poster."

Mike felt uneasy again. They'd made noise setting up their games, but now that they were through, the quiet seemed oppressive. There were a few birds singing, and a mower going on the next street, but there wasn't a shout or a scream, not a kid noise anywhere. "I don't know, but those announcements sure got us business."

"Yeah." David surveyed the games. "Well then, let's do the announcements."

They printed ten notices in red crayon, then set off on their bikes. The neighborhood up close was even more silent than it had seemed from Mike's back lawn. The imposing houses stood protected behind winding driveways, their draperied windows staring at the boys. The perfect grass and geometric flower beds were as motionless as magazine photos. "Geez, with such big houses, you'd think there'd have to be some kids," David whispered, worried for the first time.

Mike hardly heard, for he was too busy searching for the signs--a trike on a drive, some toy on a lawn. Finally, on an elbow of black asphalt, he saw a boy's bike, a golden ten-speed with tires thin as the lines on the announcements. He motioned David to come along. Mike rang the bell, waited, then rang the bell again. A young woman was wandering down a long hallway, peering at them through the bevelled glass panes beside the front door. "Would your son be interested in coming to our carnival?" Mike asked, thrusting an announcement through the opening door.

"It's gonna be the World's Greatest Carnival," David announced.

"I'm sure he would...." she began to say.

"Great! Tell him to bring lots of money," David put in.

"...if he were in town," she finished.

"He's not? But...." Mike looked back toward the bike.

The woman laughed at his bewilderment. "He left it there before he went to camp last week. We're trying to teach him a lesson, and we're hoping it rains like hell before he gets home." She stopped and searched the boys' faces. "But that's not your problem," she continued. "Well, he'll be back in three weeks. Why don't you stop by then?" She returned the announcement.

Four houses away, David spied a skateboard on the lawn. He pointed it out to Mike and together they raced across the perfect grass. David got to the doorbell first. A man in a summer business suit and tie answered. "Would your kids be interested in coming to our carnival?" the boys asked in unison.

"Our kids," the man said, wrinkling his nose a bit at their choice of the word, "are at tennis lessons. After that, they go to the club for a swim. But they should be home on the five o'clock bus." He walked around the boys to his car.

So there were still ten papers to be distributed. They rode until they saw a large new swing set in a yard, stuffed a paper in the mailbox and rode on. "That was easy," Mike said.

When they'd pushed the rest into nine other mailboxes, they began to ride back, shouting the news about the world's greatest carnival. But the only response was the droning of the air conditioning units behind the houses. Then, close to Mike's house, they passed a power vacuum following a tractor. The men on the machines, in matching brown uniforms with green pocket patches, waved to the boys.

Mike looked at his watch. It was only nine thirty. "We have a whole half hour. What should we do now?"

"I don't know. Let's see, we have the games set up and the drinks made and the popcorn...."

"Oh, geez, the popcorn!" Mike began to pedal furiously, with David in his wake, shouting, "You're gonna lose me!"

Promptly at ten, three boys appeared on Mike's drive. One had a moustache; one had a cigarette; all were a head taller than Mike and David. They looked bored. "Let's see this carnival," Moustache demanded.

David edged closer to Mike, saying as firmly as he could, "Sure, come around back."

Mike led the way, but they had barely gotten around the garage when Cigarette observed, "This don't look like no Disneyland." His friends snickered.

They all stared at David, who shrugged his shoulders. "Well, what did you expect?" David asked, sounding hurt and confused. "I only wanted to get people's attention."

"Then you should of picked another picture, 'cause everybody's been to Disneyland, so when you show that castle, everybody thinks...

you know." The boy pushed the hot red tip of his cigarette at David, who backed away. Then, laughing with his friends, the boy took an impressively long drag and exhaled slowly.

"How about popcorn?" Mike broke in, putting his hand through David's bent arm.

"Sure, that's the best idea I've heard yet," said the third boy, not very enthusiastically. "How much?"

Shaking off Mike's hand, David said, a little too loudly, "Ten cents a bag."

"Here," said the boy, shoving a bill at David. David looked at the green paper. "It's a five," he whispered.

Mike dug in his pockets. "Do you have change?" he whispered back. "All I have is some pennies for the game."

"You have to be kidding," David returned.

"Well, ah sorry, but you're our first customers and we don't...." Mike handed back the bill. "But if you can come back later...."

Together, the three boys turned abruptly, starting back around the garage. "See you in Disneyland!" Moustache called over his shoulder. David and Mike could hear them laughing all the way down the block.

And then they began to wait. Mike sold David a bag of popcorn on credit. He tried to sell some of the drink mix, but David waved it away, sinking into thoughts he refused to share. The wind pushed David's target over, and Mike made a great production of setting it back up. Eventually, David agreed to walk around to the front of the house to wait on the drive.

At last, a lanky teenager in pink shorts pulled up on a bicycle. Strapped into the yellow plastic seat on its back was a little girl, about four years old. A slightly older boy on a bike with training wheels followed close behind. "Is this the house with the carnival?" the older girl asked. "There was a flyer in the mailbox."

"See," said Mike, nudging David. "I told you. It's starting to work."

"Are these your kids?" David asked.

The girl began to laugh. "No, I'm the babysitter. Their mother thought this would be an easy way for me to keep them shut up while she napped."

The little girl had hopped out of the seat. "Take me to your thing," she commanded. With her brother and the sitter training, she followed the boys to the back lawn.

"This is the coin toss," Mike said, waving his arms around as he'd once seen a barker do it at State Fair.

"We invented it ourselves," David added, seating himself on the grass near the birdbath. "I'll make sure this one doesn't get wrecked before it's used," he explained, pointing at the cardboard target.

The little girl yawned.

"Don't you want to know how it works?" Mike asked her.

She nodded slightly.

"See, you stand behind this line and you pitch pennies into those bowls," Mike explained, looking around the side of the garage for more customers. "If you get a penny into the bowl with the five...."

"Why do I have to stand at this old string?" The little girl stamped on the string, then took a big step over it. "Why can't I stand here?"

"Because you're supposed to stand here," Mike told her patiently, jumping behind the string to demonstrate. He looked to the sitter for help, and then to David. But his friend was busy inspecting his target from the new angle, and the sitter was staring at the little boy.

"Well, I'm standing here!" Without moving, the little girl turned to the babysitter. "Gimme some money," she said. The sitter handed Mike a dime and he gave the little girl five pennies. She tossed a penny into the tub, missing the bowls, then began to walk away, asking, "What's next?"

"Well, you try again," said Mike, taking her gently by the shoulders to turn her around.

She shook him off angrily.

Mike continued, as if he hadn't noticed, "For your dime, you get five whole tries, and if you can get--let's say--twenty-five points, you'll get a prize."

"We decided a hundred points," David called over. "Do you want to run out of prizes?"

"What are the prizes?" the sitter inquired as if she cared.

Distracted by what he took for enthusiasm, David turned his attention her way. "All kinds of really great prizes!" he told her, rising from the grass. "Better than last year." He walked over to the box of prizes beneath the picnic table. With a flourish, he unwrapped the doll and held it up. "Like this one!" he exclaimed proudly.

"Oh," said the babysitter. "Well, she doesn't really need another of those, so you can save it for somebody else, but she'll play anyway. We can't be back till one."

So the little girl stood and tossed penny after penny, missing the tub most of the time. It had taken hours of discussion to settle on five throws for a dime, yet the little girl didn't seem to be keeping track. She just kept pitching pennies and the babysitter kept feeding Mike dimes. David sat on the picnic bench, watching silently as Mike made change for the sitter's bills with her own coins.

Mike walked over to the picnic table. "Let's get her to try your beanbag toss," he whispered to David. "This isn't any fun."

David was staring at the little girl, who was still tossing pennies, completely ignoring Mike's defection. "It's not like last year," he said. Then he stopped and looked at the money his friend was clutching. "Still, if she wants to pay for it...." He began to smile.

Mike abandoned the picnic table and strolled back to the sitter. "Would you like her to try one of the other games?" he asked.

"Would you like to try one of the other games?" the sitter repeated.

"This is okay," the little girl responded, but suddenly her arm was still.

Mike noticed the little boy, who was now clutching the sitter's leg. "Hey, how about you?" he asked, forcing himself to sound hearty. He gestured violently at David, who took one look at the little girl's motionless arm and jumped off the bench.

"Why, sure he wants to try a game," David began, picking up his friend's tone. "Well, young man, what'll it be, the beanbag toss or the good ol' blow-out-the-candle contest?"

"The candle game's for older kids," Mike hissed. "Don't forget how it ended up last year when we let...."

"Well, this here's an older kid," David responded, warming to his chore. He threw his arm around the boy's shoulder.

The boy twisted away with a cry and hid behind the sitter.

The little girl was watching her brother, mouth open.

Taking in the scene, David ran for the pitcher and popcorn. "Hear ye, hear ye. Ice cold drinks and popcorn, ten cents each," he proclaimed.

"Gimme some lemonade," the little girl demanded.

"Well, it's not exactly lemonade. It's lemon drink," Mike said slowly. "You know, with sugar and...."

"Their mother only lets them drink lemonade," the babysitter stated. "She buys it frozen."

Mechanically, the little girl started up again, but slower now. David stood over her, urging her on with shouts of "Thataway, kid!" After every fifth penny, he put his hand out for more money without looking at its source.

Mike poured himself a glass of the lemon drink, then, ignoring their coin box, he went with his glass to the far end of his lawn and sat down.

Promptly at 12:45, the sitter stood up and brushed off her shorts. She took the children by the hand. The little girl made no objection. "Well, thank you for having us," the sitter told David.

Before they were around the garage, Mike got up and began to pull the unlit candles out of the bottles. "What're you doing?" David asked. "It's not even one o'clock. Your mom's meeting isn't over till four."

Mike piled his soup bowls on the grass and tipped over the washtub. "We might as well clean up," he muttered. "Nobody's coming."

"Maybe those three guys are coming back. I'll go check," David called, running for the drive.

Mike crushed the cardboard target with his foot and tossed it into the trash can. David returned. "I guess you're right," he said cheerfully.

"I guess that's it." Mike was sitting on top of the picnic table, eating from a bag of popcorn. The other bags surrounded him, some falling over, but he did not notice.

"That's not it," David objected, setting a bag upright.

"What do you mean?" Mike asked listlessly.

David began to laugh. "We haven't counted our cash. I mean, what's this all about?"

Mike took another bag of popcorn and began to eat from it. "It wasn't like last year, was it?"

David was making piles of money on the picnic table. "I guess not!" he responded enthusiastically. "Look at this!"

Mike was staring at the birdbath.

David whistled his excitement and waved a five dollar bill at his friend's back. "Hey, remember this morning when we couldn't even...." He dug in again and brought out two more fives and a clot of ones. "Mike, hey, look here," he called, whistling again.

"How much?" the other asked politely.

"A heck of a lot more than last year. More than twenty five dollars."

"You aren't for real?" Mike swung around. "She didn't throw that many pennies, did she?"

David began to laugh. "Her? No. See, what happened was, at the end the lady gave me those bills and I told her I couldn't make change."

"But you had enough."

"What?"

"You cheated them!" Mike threw the bag of popcorn at him.

"No I didn't. She said it was okay. She said their mom told her to spend it all."

"But next year we can't...."

"Next year we'll have it here again, I'll tell you that much!" David put all the money back in the cash box and closed the lid with a snap.

"But I thought...."

David bent to pick up the half-full popcorn bag from the grass. "If we clean up sugar-good, your mom'll let us."

"But next year, it's your turn. When we talked on the phone, you didn't even want to have it here this year."

"But I was wrong. It was better here."

"Better?" Mike picked up an armload of popcorn bags and began to walk toward the house. Suddenly, he whirled and faced David, who had taken the pitcher and was following close behind. "It's got to be at your house next year," Mike said passionately. "I want it to be at your house next year. I want to go to your neighborhood. That's where it's... better. Let's agree right now. Next year, the carnival's at your house."

David glanced at Mike, glanced over his shoulder at the cash box on the picnic table, at the places where the games had been. "I'll have to talk to Jerry," he said finally. "Eddie too. I can't tell you right now, anyhow. It's just too far away."

What Is Forever?

"SHUT THAT BOOK AND LOOK AT THE SCENERY! WE MIGHT NOT come this way again."

Dan's sudden, familiar anger made Carol stop examining the fuzz on the edges of her sheepskin gloves. Behind her, she could hear their sons abandoning Curious George.

For thirty miles now there had been nothing beyond the car window but scrawny pines, made shorter by the drifts of February snow. And, lately, in between the trees, billboards that screamed at her about last summer's glories in the Wisconsin Dells. The whiteness of the snow was newsworthy; in the city, the snow at the roads' edges was always a Dalmatian black and white. Still, the billboards were old, hardly competition for the monkey and the Man in the Yellow Hat, as interpreted to Joe by Danny, whose single semester of first grade learning made the entertainment less reading than creative guessing.

Anyway, Carol thought, those Amazing Amphibious Ducks, and the Genuine Indian Pow-Wow! (Souvenirs Available), and even the 25 Varieties of Pancakes--all FRESH--had undoubtedly been put to sleep by now.

Put to sleep? Why choose those words? Why was she allowing Dan's mood to kill off her weekend before it began?

She'd been so bored. It always came in winter, but this year it was worse. Was it because her job had finally declined into manageable routine? Because money was so tight this year? Because the kids did not lean on her so often any more?

When Dan had come home from work with the news that someone's weekend place was theirs to use for free, she'd seen at once that these days in the country were the brief escape she'd prayed for. And the price was right. Caught up in her delighted acceptance, Dan had told her about the roads there'd be for both of them to wander, the room for Danny and Joe to play. Plans like this were part of what she loved in Dan--plans to get her into places she'd never think of by herself, and then to share them. He had been so pleased--in January.

Then why had he been so sharp with the boys just now, and over a boring stretch of outdated scenery? What lay ahead to make him so nervous? It was an old, old habit: whenever Dan was nervous, he grew sharp. Once, twice, and it passed. She supposed there were old habits of hers Dan saw but she did not.

Dan turned off the Interstate. Now they were winding between hillsides covered with snow so deep that the whiteness was broken only by the tops of cornstalks, their brown leaves waving like banners. Inside, the car was warm, but Carol realized as she watched the sharp sunshine and the brilliant blue sky that it would be very cold when they got to the vacation cabin.

Dan was looking grimmer at each turning. They were leaving the fields now, and coming into a steeper area where thick lines of trees chopped the properties into small squares. Most of the trees were barren. The car dipped down a hill and was coming up the next when Dan swore, too softly for the boys to hear. Ahead, cars lined both shoulders of the road from the crest of the hill almost to the dip ahead of them. Because of the way the road twisted, it was hard to tell if Dan could get through. And the large scale map of this county which could give them alternate routes was sitting at home, thanks to her, a fact that Dan had been bringing up with increasing frequency and bitterness.

Now they were at the cars, now worming through them. Carol took inventory. Mostly these weren't cars at all, but pickup trucks, mostly old, mostly pitted with rust. The few cars were old too.

At the top of this hill was a small white church, a classic square of wood and windows and green roof and cupola. "I bet they're having some kind of lunch, or an auction," Carol said, hoping her forced cheeriness might patch whatever ailed Dan as it always had before. It's time for this to end, she thought, more than time.

But Dan growled, "This might be the road. Here, take Tom's map." He thrust a handrawn map at her. "If I hadn't kept it in my pocket, you'd've left it home too."

Dan had stopped, waiting for directions, leaving them like a cork plugging the road, for down the next hill, all the way to the next bend, more trucks and cars lined both shoulders. Dan's fingers drummed against the steering wheel, and the sound and his anger stretched so tight that Carol longed to release her own feelings in a string of shouting. Only the thought that a speeding car might wipe them all away made her funnel her anger into a curt, "It's this one."

Dan swung left. The bag that held their meals lurched toward her. The car dipped down and up the new road three times, then stopped in front of a gate marked "Johnson." There was an old farmhouse a block from the road, but fresh snow covered any drive or sidewalk there might have been.

Dan got out and pulled their toboggan from the roof of the car. He opened the back door and called to the boys, "How about giving me a hand with all this junk. Your mother's packed us like we'd have a drive-up window." Despite the words, he was smiling.

The rage Carol had felt at the church rose up again. How could he turn it on and turn it off so fast, she wondered. Troubled, she pulled out the sack of food and started after the other three, who were already cheerfully hauling the first load of belongings across the snow.

When she reached the house, they were already inside. She stood for several minutes, inspecting the weathered grey wood siding and the sagging front porch. Dan came out first and, seeing the direction of her eyes, called down, "Come on inside. I'll start the oil stove."

"It's not what I expected," she said tightly, softly, so Joe and Danny wouldn't hear. "You said a weekend cottage."

"I said, 'place,'" Dan protested. "But you'll like it." He started toward her.

Just then Joe called; Dan turned toward the sound.

Reluctantly, Carol moved into the house. Inside, in the main room, browning wallpaper still clung to the walls, and here and there a disconnected gas fixture or a family picture punctuated faded flowers. A large, brown, metal heating stove protruded into the room. Dan was crouched in front of it, with Danny and Joe watching as if this was part of the morning's entertainment. "Here, read me the instructions," Dan demanded, shoving a paper at Carol.

"All the comforts of home," she muttered. Shrugging, she read.

The stove caught, and by the time they'd made another trip to the car, the house was so warm that Carol shed her coat. Then she wandered into the kitchen, expecting to find the same shopworn chaos. Instead, she was greeted by bright white walls, sun streaming through a neatly curtained window, a teapot on the stove and beside it a collection of teas and instant coffees and hot chocolate. Her spirits lifting, she took the teapot to the sink and turned a faucet. Nothing. "What happened to the water?" she called to Dan. There was no answer. But outside, just beyond the sunny window, she heard a throbbing sound begin, then Danny piped, "Hey, Mom, come and look!"

She stepped through the side door. Hugging herself for warmth, she looked toward the sound and found Dan standing at the base of a windmill tower, staring upward. The sound was coming from a generator attached to the pump at the base of the tower. Water was running into a large jug at Dan's feet. Above him, now, came shouts of joy. Danny had climbed nearly to the top of the tower, while Joe, younger and more timid, was clinging halfway down, trying to look jaunty.

As Dan stooped to cap the jug and move another beneath the flow of water, he called to Carol, "See, I told you." He was smiling broadly.

She supposed she should give in, go with the majority. She returned through the kitchen, through the living room, to the bedroom. Here, in addition to one double bed, two cots hugged the outside walls. Dan had already parcelled out their sleeping bags. She did not hear Dan come into the room, did not realize he was there until she felt his hand on her shoulder. He pointed to a small wood stove in one corner of the room. "If it gets too cold tonight, I can light that one too."

"Terrific," Carol said. She could not make herself sound enthusiastic. She thought about her survey of the house--kitchen, parlor, bedroom. "Where's the bathroom in this place?" she asked.

A corner of Dan's mouth dropped. "Outside," he said, and she could hear the nervous anger flicker for a moment. She followed him into the kitchen. He pointed across the sink, out the window, toward a small shed half a block away.

"Did you know about what wasn't here?" Carol demanded.

"I thought what was here might be more important. Look, we're here. The kids are happy. Can we have some lunch?"

It took some minutes to find the pots and plates and plates and utensils, more time to warm the chili on the unfamiliar stove. When Carol stepped onto the front porch to call them in, the boys and Dan had worn a toboggan run into the side of the hill that sloped away from the farmhouse.

At lunch, the boys and Dan were full of plans for the afternoon, full of ideas for a toboggan steeplechase. Carol thought the chili tasted metallic; no one else noticed the food. When they were through, the boys squirming in their seats, impatient to be outside, Dan waved them off. In the quiet, then, Dan said, "You look like a lady in need of a vacation. Would you complain if I did the dishes?"

"And what would I do?"

"Anything you want. But I promised the kids...."

"Yes, sure." Feeling rebuffed, Carol retrieved her jacket and gloves from the livingroom and stepped outside. Danny was giving Joe instructions about how to sit on the toboggan. "Want to try it, Mom?" Joe called.

Carol looked at the steep path they had carved into the snow and shook her head. Before she could say her answer, they were flying down the hillside.

She walked out past their car. She badly wanted to turn back, to ask Dan to share her walk as he had promised, but pride made her continue down the gravel road, her eyes following her shuffling feet. At the first dip, though, she remembered the crowd at the church. With a purpose, now, her step quickened, her eyes lifted, and she began to look right and left, over the banks of packed snow a plow had pushed aside. But it was only at the crossroad that she could see clearly across the fields, and there it was beautiful. Squares of white, edged by trees. Little red barns and white houses in the distance, like the plastic buildings on a

Monopoly board. And here and there the S of a road, gravel tan spotted with snow the sun had not yet cleared away. Nothing moved; there was no sound. Carol was entirely alone. She wished that Dan was here to see it, to help her savor it, to say too, "Look at that!" She could not remember a time when she had felt so alone before.

The crowd at the church had disappeared. A single car remained. Perhaps, she thought, there might be someone inside who could solve the mystery. She climbed the seven steps to the churchyard, and there she found the red clay mound of the new grave, nestled in the curve between the building and the sidewalk. "Nelson," said the large ornate letters across the top of the rose-colored double headstone. Beneath this, in a space shaped like a waving banner, "Together Forever." And then a rectangle beneath and to the left of the banner, "Rev. Martin Nelson, 1908-1979." A cross separated this from a rectangle to the lower right, and that space said, "Beloved Wife, Mary, 1918- ." The newly turned clay stretched forward below the message with the blank. "Oh, look!" Carol exclaimed into the silence, but Dan was not there to see.

Carol walked down the steps, glancing once at the peaceful scene across the road from the church. Then she returned slowly to the farmhouse in the fading light and the deepening chill that she was only now beginning to feel. The winter sun had disappeared by the time she got back, but the boys begged her to watch them take the hill once more. Her back to the house, her eyes on the toboggan, Carol felt someone nudge her shoulder. It was Dan, his arms full of wood for the bedroom stove. As soon as she acknowledged him, he disappeared into the house.

The parlor was warm. Dan had set the table for dinner; Carol could smell the food. She waited for his words to tell her if this morning's tensions had lifted, but all her men were silent, worn out by the day. Danny fell asleep over his stew, disregarding his status, and Joe, as if he'd noticed and agreed, was nodding. They carried the boys to the cots and eased them into their sleeping bags. Dan looked at the big double bed. "It'll be warmer if I zip ours together," he told her. Searching his face, Carol could not tell whether to take the words as romantic or simply practical. She started toward the kitchen and the dirty dishes.

Later that evening, they crept into the separate worlds of the books they'd brought along. Much later, Dan got the bedroom wood stove going, and turned down the oil spaceheater, then, almost wordlessly, afraid of waking their sons, Dan, then Carol, slipped into the double sleeping bag.

Dan was asleep almost at once, as asleep as Joe and Danny. Carol had always envied him this talent. For an hour or more, she lay on her half of the bed, arms tight to her sides, trying to relax, yet feeling imprisoned by the sleeping bag. She put one arm outside, but drew it back quickly. Though the pipe that climbed out of the little stove glowed red, the warmth it promised was almost entirely psychological.

Now, Carol realized, she had to get up and go to the outhouse. She lay and argued with her bladder, but in the end she rose and threw on her jacket and pulled on her boots. Dan groaned slightly at her going.

Through the parlor she went, through the kitchen, then out the side door, which seemed closer to the little shed. It occurred to her that she had not yet turned on her flashlight, and she looked up to find the reason. She could not see a moon. But every star seemed as bright as a moon against the endless blackness, and there were thousands of stars. It was peaceful, very peaceful, far more peaceful than in the city. But it was also very cold. Carol finished quickly, and returned quickly to the house.

And found the side door locked.

The night was soundless; the stars were cold and white. Carol forced herself to think. She remembered the front door. The front door was locked.

She remembered that there were no socks beneath her boots, nothing beneath her coat but a nightgown. A cold wind blew beneath her gown as she thought of it. And the sheepskin gloves were turning out to be no protection against the wind. And her face felt raw. And when she sucked in her breath, icy pins held her nostrils together.

She pounded on the front door. In the soundless night, the pounding was very loud. She felt helpless, foolish, but almost immediately the certainty of her peril drowned the other thoughts. She prayed that Dan would hear. Would rescue her.

He came, not surprised, not laughing at her plight, not angry, just half asleep. By the time she had taken off her coat and gloves and boots, he had crept back into the sleeping bag.

She glanced at each of her sleeping sons, then slid into the bag beside Dan. As she rolled away from the cold metal of the zipper, she felt his arm come out to pull her home. The warmth radiated from him in a circle, like the yellow of a sunflower. She did not know how long she had been gone. She only knew that the flannel on her side of the double bag was now far colder than the space near Dan. His eyes were closed, but his arm remained outstretched toward her.

She stared at the ceiling and thought about the day. She thought about Dan's anger, about their sons' pleasure. She thought of Mary Nelson, now, beneath the new mound of clay, beside Martin in the unopened snow.

Mary had been ten years younger than her Martin, with so much time to be left behind. Yet time had brought her luck. It had only left her....Carol's sleepy mind subtracted. Four years.

She thought of how four years would be for her, if death wrenched Dan away. It would be as if someone had torn off half her self. She thought of Dan lying there, silenced, and how she might call out, "Wait, oh wait...one more thing I never told you...you must know....." And they had been together such short years, while Mary and her Martin....

But did Mary want it so? Carol pictured the stone. Beloved wife, the stone had said. Together forever, the stone had said. The stone was carved to Mary's order; left behind, she shaped the words, the wish.

Carol wondered then about Mary's life alone. Had they been kind to her, his flock, as kind as to their pastor? She remembered the lines of cars and trucks. Lucky Mary, yes.

Dan sighed in his sleep. Carol's mind shifted to the anger that had all but destroyed the morning, that had colored and shaded so much of the rest of the day. Dan had known how much she looked forward to this weekend, and had at least suspected how imperfect things might be here. Perhaps his anger had been born of anxiety for her happiness, or perhaps it grew from guilt about what he hadn't mentioned, flaws that, in the long run, were so minor, yet would have seemed major enough at home to keep her there. She'd seen both kinds of anger in him before this.

No! her mind shouted at her. No! You cannot go on excusing him forever. You cannot go along enduring this.

But he endures your panics, said her mind. And surely, he likes them no more than you appreciate his angers.

The thought stopped her. For as long as she had known Dan, he had never laughed at her, no matter how absurd she must have seemed. And when she panicked, as she had just now, he never grew impatient. He had only always been there. But how must he feel?

The warmth of Dan's side of the sleeping bag was drawing her closer. There were some things that were forever. Like Death.

But some things could be changed, must change. While there was time. Time to say. Saying was not a cure, but it was a beginning. And she and Dan had time.

She let his warm arm pull her further from the chill at her edge of the bed.

The Stranger

SHE WAS SO WHITE, MARGE WOULD TELL GREG WHEN HE GOT home from Honolulu. From her freshly set hair, to her starched uniform, to her stockings and her polished orthopedic oxfords, the frail elderly lady was all white, except for the red trademark embroidered on her left lapel. And the curious antique leather valise she carried, which seemed to have no opening. The valise was dark brown.

Marge would tell Greg how the lady's expression had broadened into joy when the front door opened, and how the lady's heels had started bouncing in anticipation.

"Now, if only you could think of cleaning that way...." Greg said, then he began to laugh. It was Sunday. They were standing in the basement. And something in that place had changed.......

Fits of neatness eventually attacked Greg if he stayed home long enough. He'd need a break from the project he was doing at his workbench, so he'd take a stroll around the basement and spot their storage shelves. And howl.

Their daughters knew that howl by heart. It meant that in three minutes he would be in their room, demanding that they clean. Their record for clearing out of the house post-howl was to minutes and fourteen seconds, but they were working at improving that time. Marge's speech about how the basement was their mutual mess needed no improvement. It never failed to remind Greg that he had other things to do.

It was odd the way Marge had found the elderly lady's employer. Last Monday morning, she had been in the basement, searching for her grandmother's noodle board. The board was not for noodles, but for Janet, her neighbor, who had a needlepoint canvas to stretch and block. Marge would have believed that noodles grew in cellophane bags on pasta bushes, except that, once her mother had brought her this outsize board, neatly wrapped and labelled.

Marge thought she saw a sharp corner in dusty brown paper sticking out beneath the huge roasting pan she used for the Thanksgiving turkey every other year. But the roasting pan was underneath four tall stacks of <u>Popular Mechanics</u> magazines that Greg was saving in case he put together enough days off to do a few more projects. The roaster was oval, though, so the two outside stacks were not quite horizontal. The collection had a habit of shifting uneasily if someone tiptoed by.

Nevertheless, a large carton rested on top of the magazines. It was a bright yellow carton, with an English Beefeater guard strolling across its side. The name of the gin had been crossed out with a heavy black pen and the words "Marge's personal junk" put in its place. It was Greg's handwriting, put there after Marge had labelled a light green carton, its flaps flung open, its top mounded high, "Greg's garbage."

Marge put her right hand on the corner of the noodle board, laid her left palm against the piles of magazines, recited her favorite prayer to the Law of Inertia, and pulled the board. Ordinarily, this system worked, but on Monday, the pile in question had come clattering and fluttering and clunking down around her, and the mounds on the other shelves quivered dangerously until she glared them into submission.

Then, just when she thought the earthquake had ended, Greg's uncle's Prohibition-era, heavy-gauge steel bottle-capper came flying end over end from the top of the highest of the piles and landed five inches from her left heel. The newspaper it had been more or less wrapped in unwound itself as the capper plummeted, then found its way into his right hand, which she had been holding over her face to ward off the capper.

And that was how the Rent-A-Stranger service came to Marge's attention.

"Tired of contending with the memories in your basement?" the advertisement asked, as if it had just witnessed the scene. Then it explained how, for a small fee, Marge could hire one of their Strangers to come into her house. "It's all junk to us," the ad continued merrily. But just as Marge decided that the idea was too coldhearted to consider, some printing she had not noticed before reassured her that if she hadn't seen the stuff in years, it probably wouldn't kill her to never see it again.

When Marge shifted a little, her foot grazed the heavy bottle-capper. She looked again at the last words, reflecting that although the ad's copywriter probably hadn't meant the message literally, one piece had almost killed her within the past five minutes.

The ad concluded with a telephone number but, oddly, no address. Marge called, and on Tuesday, the elderly little lady was standing on her doorstep bouncing up and down. Two days before the girls returned from summer camp. Five mornings before Greg was due home from the seminar in Hawaii. And well before Marge could reconsider.

It was odd the way the fragile little lady seemed to know where she was headed. Marge followed her down the basement steps, past the washer and dryer, past the pool table, directly to the shelves. Marge was amazed that someone so old and frail could walk so briskly.

The lady put her leather valise down then, like a miner, inspected the shelves, considering where to start chipping away.

Then the lady nodded to herself, reached up and plucked a photo album from a pile Marge would have sworn was several feet too high for her to reach. She dangled it between her thumb and forefinger, well away from her immaculate white uniform. The pages of the album, moist from years of storage in the damp basement, drooped. Though Marge could not remember whose pictures these were, she still felt guilty about allowing the Stranger to dispose of people's past. She wondered why the lady was taking so much time with the album, almost displaying it. If each item took this many minutes, she'd be boarding the lady for the rest of the year.

Just then, a wiggling furry creature slithered from between the album's pages and dropped onto the floor. Without thinking, Marge stomped the bug.

"Quite right," the Stranger said, as if Marge had spoken her permission. Then she laid the book on top of the valise and in an instant, the album had disappeared. There was no grinding sound, or burning smell. The damp pages and the mildewed cover were simply gone.

Marge gasped. The lady looked at her, frowning. "Did they not tell you when you called the service? You mayn't stay here, or else you'll find me gone." The voice was far, far younger than the face.

Yesterday, Marge had pushed the bottle-capper back into the chaos of the top shelf, but now it began to rock slightly, although there was no movement nearby, and no breeze in the room. The rocking began an avalanche of old papers, which fell around Marge and fed her desperation. "But you aren't going to...uh...take it all?" Marge cried out. "Look, I know that some of these boxes are almost empty." She gestured at the fifty-odd boxes on the shelves. "I mean, while you're neatening things up, couldn't you save some of the things?"

"The things you need, we leave."

"But how are you supposed to know what I need if I don't stay and tell you?"

Trust me.

When Marge thought back, and she'd have cause to think back many times, she could not recall the last words being spoken. And yet she knew she'd heard them the moment she found herself at the top of the basement stairs, heading for her living room. And the oddest part was, she did trust the Stranger.

An hour later, Marge came upon the little lady as she was slipping out the back door. Her hair still looked freshly set. Her shoes were unsmudged. The sharp creases in her unsoiled uniform were still in place. Her small hands, very clean, held the strange antique valise ahead of her.

"But where's the garbage? Did you bag it? Do I bring it up myself?"

"There is no garbage," the Stranger answered, sounding slightly insulted. "Our work is guaranteed." And then she added just one word, "Forever," and her heels began to bounce.

A noise in the other room distracted Marge. When she turned back, the elderly Stranger was her valise were gone.

Janet did not show up for the noddle board until Thursday. She had the canvas in her hand as if to show how anxious she was to finish her project.

Marge had not gone to the basement after the Stranger left, afraid that she would be disappointed. But when she went down to look for the board, she took a moment to glance around, and what she saw pleased her immensely. There were no more loose piles of anything, and about half the boxes were gone too. The Stranger had apparently found room in the remaining cartons for everything worth keeping. Not a single box top bulged.

Light shone onto the shelves through two windows that for years had been covered with curtains of assorted things. The window panes were newly washed, inside and out. Marge looked around for the rags the lady had used, but these, too, were missing. Uneasily, Marge recalled the way the valise had eaten up the photo album; she did not think the rage could have been stored in the valise.

The noddle board was underneath a bright yellow carton. Marge could not remember leaving two of these cartons, yet the original, the one with Greg's angry printing on it, and gone.

The roasting pan was also gone. Only one <u>Popular</u> <u>Mechanics</u> remained lying on top of the closed yellow carton. Curious to discover why the Stranger had chosen this issue to leave, Marge flipped through to the projects page.

Janet called down the steps, pretending concern about Marge's welfare. Forget you, Marge thought, for she suddenly recalled that the final stitches had been put into Janet's needlepoint three months before.

The project in this issue had been a phenomenally intricate combination bookcase, record cabinet and television stand that folded out into a wet bar and complete miniature kitchen. The diagrams seemed to call for several million tiny pieces of wood. Marge recalled the seven projects, each half-done, each abandoned, that already lay scattered on Greg's workbench, the projects that brought knots of anger to her stomach whenever she saw them and bitter words when Greg was home to hear them. And those projects had been child's play compared to this one. Well, Marge thought, you really goofed on this one, Stranger.

But again the silent voice begged Marge's trust.

When Janet called down the steps this time, Marge could hear, behind her voice, the sound of her daughters' camp bus pulling up in front of the house. She closed the magazine and was about to put it on top of the yellow carton when she noticed that the cover advertised an article called, "Choosing Your New Station Wagon." She recalled that at the airport, just before Greg had to board his plane, he'd talked about buying a station wagon. "To do more things together," he had said, then left her wondering how he meant to do that, when his job stole him from her so many days of every year.

Besides, they could not afford a new station wagon. Goofed again, Lady, she muttered, and shook her head.

Then she took a second look at the cover. The magazine was three years out of date.

On Sunday, Greg returned, leaving his suitcase full of dirty clothes at the bottom of the basement steps.

As he always had for the six years he'd run these far-flung seminars, he sat in his lounge chair and slipped into the post-trip recollections. He talked about the overpriced and underseasoned food at his hotel, the days of playing mental tug-of-war with the half of the group that thought they were in Hawaii on vacation. He talked about the lonely nights. And all the while, he lay back in his chair, his eyes half-closed.

"You haven't told me about the beach yet," Marge had intended to make a joke, but she could hear the bitter edge. Greg sat up and caught her eyes.

But then he laughed, I could have been in Alaska, for all I saw of it."

She looked at the pale face surrounding the tired eyes, and trusted him.

"But I did find the time to buy you a souvenir. It's in my suitcase."

"I wish you hadn't." Marge words were out before she thought about them. He'd ask her now, and after six years of pretending otherwise, how could she now tell him the truth? The souvenirs were always only bits of jewelry, or dresses. But the message to her in each one had been that he'd been gone, and she had missed him, and he'd soon be gone again. She detested the souvenirs, even the pretty ones, and had stored

129

them quickly in a large, flat coat box on a bottom basement shelf. Because she had overdone her thanks, though, Greg never seemed to notice that she never wore his gifts.

Marge bent over the back of his chair and kissed his forehead. "I missed you very much," she said, "but I should start your wash. And see what you brought me," she added hastily.

She picked up the suitcase from the basement floor, opened it on top of the dryer, and began to sort his clothes. Whatever his latest gift was, she would put it with the others. Then she would try to pretend that he'd never been away.

But when the suitcase was empty, she still had found no souvenir.

As the washer whooshed into its wash cycle, Marge scanned the shelves. With so many cartons gone, it was easy to find the coat box. She pulled it onto the floor and opened it.

It was completely empty.

Then she thought about the missing roasting pan. It had been expensive; she wondered why the Stranger had taken it--or whatever it was that she had done with it. Marge was beginning to feel slightly uncomfortable because she could not find a word that quite described what she suspected the little lady had done with all her things.

And then she thought about the times the roaster had been used. She thought about the tension, from the moment she'd started defrosting the enormous turkey to the moment the twenty other members of Greg's family departed, never saying thanks.

But that memory was not quite accurate. Actually, the tension always lasted several days beyond Thanksgiving. Last year, it had lasted until Greg left on his next trip.

Which was, Marge now recalled, the time of the duel of the box labels. She had come down here to put the roaster away and had opened the light stack, then restacked all those magazines. And then she'd spied the light green carton overflowing with Greg's old, useless things. And next to it the Magic Marker one of the girls had left behind....

When she looked for Greg's carton, she found one just like it, but without her label. She looked inside; the carton was less than half full.

She heard the washer kick into its rinse cycle and knew she had been standing here for almost twenty minutes.

Greg was waiting for her at the top of the steps to find out that she liked the souvenir. Marge was too tired to lie. "I didn't find it," she told him.

But when she protested that he'd left it in a little silk side pocket, she took him to the basement and, slowly, reluctantly, afraid he'd accuse her of lying, Marge told Greg about the Stranger. About her odd white uniform, and why she had been hired, how she had come and gone in just an hour, and how the picture album had disappeared into the valise. But not exactly into....

Greg did not seem angry, but puzzled. "I don't understand what this has to do with the new souvenir, though. If it's as you're telling me, she was here five days ago."

And then, ignoring the hint that he did not believe her, Marge told Greg about the lady's guarantee.

The basement air was having a tranquilizing effect on Greg. He put his arms around Marge. "That was the last souvenir anyway," he said.

"Because I...let them go?"

He laughed. "Because I have a new job. I tried to tell you before I left, but then they called my plane. As of tomorrow, I'll be the one who plans the seminars, but somebody else will have to take them on the road."

To have Greg home again full time, to talk to, to consult with, to rely on, to rely on her, or just to touch, if that became her need--it was what Marge had been hoping for ever since the aching reality of his absences had come clear to her. She supposed that she could even forgive him his basement projects. Yet all that she could do now was to ask him, "Why the change?"

"Because I missed you," he answered lightly, but he held her closer yet. "I missed your cooking and your sense of humor and...just...you. And the way you have of making up stories to cover your...."

"But, Greg, the Stranger wasn't a story," Marge protested.

Ignoring her protest, Greg continued, "It was a long flight home from Hawaii. I thought about a lot of things, things I'll have time to do now." Taking her hand, Greg led Marge to his workbench.

But the wooden top was absolutely bare, and only half his tools were hanging on the pegboard on the wall. The other half, the almost useless weird ones, were gone. And so were all seven projects.

Greg stared at the bare workbench, then took inventory of the pegboard. Marge waited for the howl, but suddenly, Greg hugged her again. "How did you know I couldn't figure out how to go on?" he exclaimed. "And how did you know that I felt guilty every time I looked at those tools I never should've bought?"

"Not me. I told you. Greg, trust me. The Stranger was no story." Marge pointed to a small white calling card that she suddenly noticed sticking up between two boards in the workbench top.

Greg took the card and read the elaborate red printing. "Where did you have this made up?" he asked.

Marge shook her head. "I didn't."

He looked again at his bare workbench, then strolled back to the shelves. "But what's left to remind us what to fight about?" he called to her. Then they both began to laugh.

A long time later, days later, Greg looked again for the calling card, for he wanted to recommend the service to a friend. He could not find it. "Where did you say that lady came from?" he asked Marge.

But the odd thing was, Marge never knew the answer.

Printed in the United States
by Baker & Taylor Publisher Services